Tough Luck

(A FORBIDDEN ROMANCE)
by Christa Simpson

Black Widow
Publishing

TOUGH LUCK
By Christa Simpson

Copyright 2015 Christa Simpson
All rights reserved.

Electronic Edition
ISBN: 978-1-926478-06-7

Paperback Edition
ISBN: 978-1-926478-07-4

Cover Design by Christa Simpson
www.christasimpson.com

Copy Editor: Intuition Author Services
www.intuitionauthorservices.blogspot.com

Publisher: Black Widow Publishing
www.BWPbooks.com

Tough Luck

Even if it means we're wantonly destroying our family . . . I can't resist him.

He tells me he can be my dark little secret and I'm honestly having a hard time saying no. When the good-girl librarian meets the wealthy bad boy with impossibly dark eyes, a beautiful chaos ensues. But what do you think happens when he's a "get what I want, when I want" kind of guy and what he wants is me?

1

Old Love

Have you ever caught your mother getting felt up by her new boyfriend? No, me either . . . until today. Let me tell you, you cannot unsee that shit. I glare across the room at the wrong kind of love unfolding in my childhood kitchen. I bet I'm frowning now, and I've only been in this house for a day. It's depressing watching my mother and her perfect little relationship with Jason.

I inwardly sigh. It's my birthday—*my* birthday—the one day a year my mother is mine. So what if they're getting married tomorrow, and who cares if my new *brothers* are supposed to arrive soon? *Not me.* I must be the only one here who realizes that they're late and I'm going out, with or without my mother.

I place the last dish in the cupboard and hang the wet dish towel over the handle of the warm stove to air-dry it. Making a quick turn for the stairs, I finally seem to get my mother's attention.

"Where are you going?" she asks.

I peer at her over my shoulder, hoping not to find her giggling with Jason's hands on her ass. "Upstairs." Which I thought was quite obvious.

"So early?"

"It's almost ten, Mom. I'm beat, and you have a big day ahead of yourself." *All true.*

"Okay, honey. Happy birthday."

"Yeah, happy," I say without thinking, knowing I'm going to get a good old lecture for this one.

My mother sighs and steps toward me, Jason taking a well-timed leave into the other room. I'm in trouble. I can see it in her eyes. Even after living on my own for two years, I can still tell when I'm going to get it. Displeasure hovers in the air between us, but strangely she doesn't strike. She looks down her nose at me, but her voice is soft and understanding.

"You said it yourself, Izzabelle. Tomorrow's a big day for me. We can go out another night."

I nod my head, while completely disagreeing with her. I know there won't be another night, and I fear that she can still read me the way she always did. A mother knows best, right? Wrong. Not this time. She's picking him over me, and that hurts. The way Jason has so quickly displaced me is disheartening and dominates my thoughts the closer their wedding gets.

My mother glances over her shoulder to make sure Jason can't hear her. I hold my breath and my body starts to tremble from the weight of this conversation. I can't shake that rotten feeling. It's like a ball of yarn has become lodged in my throat and a bunch of lead pellets are exploding in my belly, one by one. She rests her hands on my shoulders and sighs with a start.

"You're still okay with this, right?"

I can see the worry in her brow and the anxiety in her heart, just from asking me a stupid question. I don't know why I do this to her. She doesn't deserve it.

"Of course," I lie, exhaling a tired breath.

I have to lie. I love my mom. I do. And just because I feel lonely and abandoned, doesn't mean that my mom has to.

A small smile squeaks out of me, as I'm pulled into an embrace that is super tight and lasts extra-long. My heart transforms into a swollen bowling ball, pounding harshly against my chest, heavy with emotion.

"Love you, Mom," I whisper, feeling like it could be my last chance to tell her so.

Her resulting smile makes me feel guilty for what I'm about to do tonight, but it's not going to stop me. When she finally lets me go, I notice company has rejoined us, so I leave my apology to her for another time.

No, Jason, I haven't convinced her to run.

But I see the way he looks at me. He tries to hide it, but I know there's an evil eye he's fighting to restrain. I can't blame the guy. I'm the evil step-daughter who can't be trusted. I look all sweet and nice on the outside, but inside is a raving lunatic just waiting to come out. Setting all that aside, I've known my mom a lot longer than him, and she never dodges her commitments. She promised that she would go out for our celebratory drink tonight. He's changing her.

"I just wanted to go out tonight, the way we always go out," I explain, so they both believe it's not their wedding that's the problem, although it totally is.

My mom slants her head at me, in a motherly gesture that's become all too familiar over the past twenty four hours. I avoid the words I know she's going to say if I don't scale these stairs right now. I spin away as they both flash a fleeting parental look at me.

He's not my father. One parent is enough. I'm getting too old for this shit, and I really don't need this today—on my birthday.

I try not to act like a child, but my feet are so heavy that when I climb the first few steps, it sounds like I'm stomping.

Damn it! I can't hide my feelings about this wedding, even if I want to.

I hope they realize weddings aren't my thing. It's nothing against them. Well, maybe a little against Jason for stealing my mom away from me, but I have nothing against my mom.

Being lighter on my feet, I slip up the rest of the stairs and into my old room, softly shutting my door and turning over the small button on the handle, just like I used to when I was a kid. I slump my shoulders and close my eyes instantly, with too many miserable memories returning to me.

"It's for your own good, honey," my mother hollers up

the stairs, adding insult to injury.

And there it is. I rest my forehead against my door and bang it one time, instantly regretting it. I rub the sore spot and sulk while she responds again, "One day, when you're older, you'll understand."

Even though her voice softens, I hear every word and commit that tone to memory. "She'll come around," I hear her say to Jason, even though she doesn't expect me to hear her.

Well, guess what, Mom? I did! And I won't!

Pacing my old room only stresses me out further. I need to get out of here before I go mad. Shutting out my mother's advice, I toss my wide-rimmed glasses on the bed and pull on my oversized white headphones. Settling into the worn out purple beanbag chair under the window, I try to picture how tomorrow is going to go. Not good. Everyone will be smiling and even I'll have to fake how happy I am.

I turn up the music until it's earsplittingly loud, and I sink into a guitar riff from Metallica. Even with this shitty mood hanging over my head, I have to attempt my best air guitar. There's no avoiding it to this song. I smile, but it's not going to last if I sit here and do nothing. Music usually soothes me, but there will be no relaxing tonight. I flip into panic mode and jump to my feet when the realization really hits me.

My mom is getting married tomorrow!

Holy fucking shit, shitty.

I shake all thoughts of sabotage from my head and decide to continue with my plan. I'm going out tonight. By myself. No one needs to know, and no one will know, because I'll be unrecognizable. It's not like I'm a regular or even a random. I never go out. Actually, I do go out. Once a year. With my mother. On my birthday.

Since that's not going to happen, and even my girl Sadie has rejected me tonight, I will have to grow a new persona for the evening. Going in public isn't necessarily easy for me, either. Starting a conversation with a stranger isn't something I do, ordinarily. I need a change. Tonight, that'll change.

After tossing the headphones on my bed, I shuffle through my closet trying to find something inappropriate to wear. Behind my muted beige pants and modest blouses, I find a really short black dress that I haven't worn since I was sixteen. With good reason! It's short—like really short. My legs must have grown a few inches since I last saw this thing, too. I hold the skirt against my body. I can see it'll land very high on my thighs. I'll be surprised if it even covers my ass. *Perfect!*

I tear off my pants and put the thing on. Oh, I don't know if I can pull this off. I don't exactly work out, but I'm not overweight by any means. I have long enough legs. I cringe at the thought of wearing this little black thing in public. Staring at myself in the mirror, I'm forced to look at the positive things. My mother would be devastated by my selection. That fires up my resolve. I think I can pull it off. At least, here's to trying!

I fight to squeeze the zipper up on the dress, but I do it. With another squinted glance at myself in the mirror, I have to admit, I'm pretty darn happy with the result. This thing holds me in, flattens me down, and boosts me up, in all the right places, showing off my legs.

After smoothing my hand over my flattened tummy, I face away from the mirror and lean forward to check the damage. My ass cheeks practically hang out, as I suspected they would. Overboard? Maybe. One little reach across the bar will be all it takes to give the whole place a show. I guess I'd better lose these granny panties. It's time to sport something a little skimpier.

Losing the comfy white panties, I break the tags off the one and only thong I own. It's red and lacy and will ride up my ass, which is exactly why I've never worn it, but I hear it's supposed to make you feel sexy. I flip my skirt over it and look at my bent-over ass in the mirror. I guess if you think wedgies are sexy . . .

Ugh, but my face is so plain Jane. Moving closer to the mirror I gawk and scowl at every freckle. I will definitely have to do something to cover up this face, ugh, and these eyelashes! There's nothing beautiful about my boring brown hair and pale lashes. I feel like I was beat with the ordinary stick. I can't go out looking like this.

With a pout on my mouth, I swipe on some foundation that makes my face look unrecognizably clear. Next, I dig to the bottom of my makeup case where I find the blood red lipstick that I only wear for Halloween. I rub it over my lips repeatedly and smack them together until they are a vivid shade of crimson. I smile at myself, my face suddenly looking a lot more glamorous. My finger nails won't know what happened to them, either, when I swipe on the matching polish.

Wearing my oversized headphones, I wave my wet nails in the air, shaking my bare rear to my favorite beats. My breasts have always bounced, but I don't remember my ass swaying quite like this before.

Tonight will be fun.

By the time the fourth song is finished, my nails are dry, my lips are puckered and my eyelashes are full, pitch black, and curled up at the edges. I look like an expensive hooker, which is exactly what I was going for, so we're good.

I boost life into my otherwise flat hair, curling random strands with the hot iron I haven't pulled out since my eighth grade graduation. With a can of hairspray in hand, I close my eyes and hold my breath. For a few minutes I'm bathing in fumes, but hey, it smells good and it works. Once my hair is set, I crawl into my closet, hoping my one and only pair of black heels are still buried back there.

Yes!

I hold them over my head in triumph, although I never could walk in the darn things. They strap on easy enough, but I really have no idea how I'm going to wear these things all night. I scuffle over to the bed and perch my rear on the edge of it. With crossed legs, I shake my foot, waiting for my mother and her little lover to call it a night. They can't be long now, but patience has never been my strong suit.

As soon as the last of the lights turn down for the night, I slowly lift my window and pry out the screen. I honestly doubt either of them will hear anything over their giggling downstairs. It makes me sick. I know they're tumbling around in my mother's bedroom, trying to keep quiet, but they're not—not even a little bit.

That's my mom, dude. Not cool!

Don't get me wrong, I'm happy for my mother. My father was an A-hole and my mother does deserve to be happy again, but why does she have to get her happy on with me in the house? All the more reason for me to escape this place. It's true, I've considered throwing in the towel on this adventure. Twice. Still, the ticking sound of the big, round clock on the wall is deafening. The time to step up to the plate is now.

Can I do this? Hell yes!

2

Bad Girl

In all my teenage years, never have I ever climbed down my mother's trellis. Deciding now is as good a time as ever to learn how, I bury a few twenty dollar bills in my overstuffed bra and throw those damned high heels to the ground. All things considered, it's pretty easy to get through my window. No cars pass, no thorns snag my dress, and no lights turn on in the house, so I think I'm in the clear.

I drop to the damp grass, grab ahold of my shoes and boot it to my car, only a little scared to see what my mom's ivy looks like in the morning. With my shoes dangling from my left hand, I pick my car's lock with the key, as if I'm burglarizing it. My heart is racing, even though I know the odds of getting caught doing this are slim to none.

I never do stuff like this!

There's something rustling in the bushes, and my heart leaps into my throat as a large male cat slinks out from underneath it. Meeeowww, the cat howls, begging for some attention. A whoosh of air passes between my lips as I smile at him, the beginning of a nervous laugh. Then there's another sound, just beyond the tall green tangle of leaves, that makes my voice catch in my throat. My insides tighten, waiting to see what else I might run into tonight.

All I see is a small flicker of red, the burning end of a cigarette. God damn neighbors. Why do they have to hide like that? If I didn't know any better, I'd say they're spying on me. No matter what time of day it is, either him or his girlfriend is sitting on the front porch. It's like they take turns keeping watch on my mom's house.

How creepy.

I fight with my door to get it open, knowing the neighbor won't speak a word of this to my mother. He's oh so nosy, but he never makes a peep to me or my mom. I focus on the task at hand, yank open my door and drop in my seat. The ripped leather seat is still warm from the heat of the day.

It's impossible to close my ratty car door quietly, so I don't even bother trying. I turn on the car and force both of my front windows down at once, waiting for the air conditioning to kick in. It finally does when I'm parking my car at the Ophelia Lounge.

As I approach the swanky bar, sweat glistening on my neck and chest, I wonder why they even call it a lounge. I doubt much lounging goes on inside. By the look of the people standing in line and the sound of the bass echoing from the building, I imagine a lot of flirting, dancing and drinking goes on in there. I will soon find out.

Taking a quick look both ways, I hustle up to the man blocking the door, careful not to trip on a pothole and land in a mud puddle. As his eyes drive into mine, my shyness tries to encompass me, but I don't let it. I wait for him to say something, but he doesn't. I hand him my driver's license, because that seems like a smart thing to do. It's what the others in front of me did, so I imagine it's a good start.

He smirks, has a look at my license and then turns those dark eyes back on me. "Are you VIP?"

Since I have no idea what he's talking about, my smile turns sly, while I conjure up something witty to say. If I'm going to do this, I'm going to have to embrace my inner goddess. God knows she's hiding in there somewhere.

"I think I am," I say, with a prowess I didn't even know I had.

The man's eyes fall down my body, paying extra attention to my perky breasts and landing on my naked thighs. He smirks and then nods, as I slip the card back into my bra, right next to my car key. I'm in?

I'm in!

He removes the dark velvet rope, and I slip past him, pushing on the black glass door to enter the nightclub. The second I step foot inside, the room opens up like a massive auditorium, with small balconies perched above the dance floor on either side. Three levels of bars wrap around me with a mixture of socialites and scumbags lining each one. The place is packed and a hint of anxiety sneaks in before I quickly brush it away.

My eyes travel across the crowd trying to find somebody I know, with little hope. No such luck. Skipping the bar, I decide to make my way around the room and if nothing else scope out where the restrooms are. I go with the flow, passing through the crowd, smiling at strangers and flipping my primped hair.

Where has this bold woman come from? I like her!

Turning away from a handsome stud, I point toward my nose to push up my non-existent glasses, shocked by how well I can see while wearing contact lenses. Fine-looking men are everywhere: muscles, skin and bones. More like walking boners. Some of the women are taking their dancing to another level, trying to compete with the two Go-Go dancers in the cage tacked up on the far wall. Others are dressed conservatively, as if they came out directly after work, while most are minimally clothed, with tall shoes and cleavage being a common theme.

Lights flash around me, as I scope out the rest of bar area. I find a single stool flanked by a college-aged guy wearing a collared plaid shirt, and an older business-looking man in a leather jacket. I squeeze in between them and carefully tuck my skirt in at the sides, with my legs squeezed tightly together. Neither of them act like I even exist, and I am totally okay with that.

With great effort, I convince myself to be courageous. I flag down the bartender and order whatever's on tap, since that's what I heard the college guy get. The drink sloshes over the rim of my glass when he drops it in front of me. I pay the man and he instantly leaves me to help another young lady, dressed as scantily as myself.

My drink goes down quickly and the bartender hands me another one before I even ask for it.

"Thanks!" I tell him, smiling with rosy cheeks.

What? I'm happy! No one's ever bought me a drink before.

The bartender smirks, as if he knows I don't get out much. "Don't thank me," he shouts back, nodding down the bar.

I slowly draw my eyes to where he nods, terrified that my mother has followed me here. Embarrassment consumes my smile before I connect with the person sitting there, but it is not my mother. In fact, it's a guy. Not just any guy, either. He has to be the sexiest, most mysterious guy in the place, all dark-tanned skin, hidden eyes, and broad shoulders.

He's wearing a powder blue hat pulled so low that it casts shadows over his eyes, but I can still see him when he peeks up at me.

God damn!

Luck is on my side tonight. He's sitting alone, sucking on a beer bottle, buying random girls drinks?

I don't care.

He looks so enigmatic over there. Just the thought of having a conversation with him has my bottom lip trembling. He would make a good romance cover model. His facial hair is impeccably trimmed and muscles bulge from his shirt sleeves. What I'd do to wrap my hands around those arms. I wonder if it'd be inappropriate if I asked to snap a photo with him. I knew there was a reason to bring my phone.

Dammit! The girls at the library won't believe this without proof.

I can't look away, feeling so drawn to him, and with him ignoring me I decide I'm allowed to study him a little longer. Pink lips. A man with full pouting pink lips, so soft and full and kissable. He takes good care of himself. He must tan. No, with rough hands like those, he works outdoors.

My mind carries me away to imagine what it would feel like to have those big, rough hands exploring my body. The second I slip into fantasy, my entire body flushes with heat and I feel his eyes on me. Does he know I'm thinking about him? Is he thinking about me, too? I need to catch a glimpse of those eyes, but whenever I look up, he glances away.

A surge of anxiety rushes over me. I wonder if he recognizes me from the library. I know I've never seen this stud muffin before. What if he's a father from the kids' program I run there. *Oh, that would be disturbing.* I flash a quick glance at his left hand. No jewelry. It's a start.

While I'm celebrating with a smile, a man with silver grey hair next to me grins and raises his voice so I can hear him over the music. "That's not going to do it." He takes a gulp from his glass, making the clear brown liquid disappear.

Do I look like I want to talk? Cuz I don't. At least, not to him. "Pardon me?" I ask, while debating whether the silent treatment would've been a smarter decision.

The man is clearly wealthy, but has a thirst for hard liquor; not someone I want to acquaint myself with. He looks at me and a smirk tugs at the corner of his lips. "That boy over there has been staring at you ever since you walked in the door. Why don't you go over and introduce yourself? You can't do that from over here."

Why? So you can watch me from afar? Creep.

This means he has been watching me, too, and an icy feeling crawls up my spine when I wonder how many other creepers have their eyes on my ass at this very moment.

I look up from our conversation, gaze down the bar, and finally make eye contact with the mystery man. A lick of desire passes through my body like an electrical current. His eyes are even more penetrating than I had imagined—a storm of swirling darkness—and I can't look away.

He breaks the stare down first, and a relieved breath tears through my lips before I turn away. Now I definitely have to meet him. It takes a few seconds for me to regain my balance, but I gawk at the guy again, unable to peel my eyes away for fear he might disappear, even though he hasn't moved a muscle except to lift his bottle of beer. He adjusts his hat and I wonder if it's to keep his eyes hidden from me again.

What is he hiding from?

3

Thirsty

I'm feeling good after finishing the free drink, and I think I've got a handle on these shoes. Battling for bravery, I spin around and get to my feet, ready to go ask this man all the questions I've practiced in my head three times over. I strut across the room, knowing his eyes follow my path. I can feel it. It sets my body on fire as my hips sway to the rapid beat of my heart, my legs feeling a little like my favorite brand of jelly.

Suddenly, mid-stride, knowing that he's watching, I forget how to walk. I stumble over my own two feet and tumble onto all fours, skidding my knee and landing in a sticky puddle of *lord knows what* not far from his feet. My driver's license falls out of my bra and goes sliding across the grimy floor as the crowd starts to hollow out around me.

This is my worst nightmare come true. People start to point, laugh, and stare. I crawl across the floor to grab my photo ID and stuff it back to where the sun don't shine, wishing I could crawl into a hole and die. I pray that I get trampled by the dancers, while gathering enough courage to look up, but as an upbeat song ends, a snippy jack ass makes a comment that leaves me frigid.

He flips my skirt up with the toe of his shoe. *Why did I wear this stupid getup, again?* Cringing, my eyes fall back to the floor. I've got myself in a hell of a predicament here, or so I thought until a pair of big shoes walks up and stops next to me.

Look at the size of them feet! Shit is about to get real.

"Is there a problem here?" The depth of the threat in his voice sends a delicious shiver down my body. I can't see him, but I see the way the problem scurries away and how the other men wither into the darkness.

It's him. It's him! I know it's him.

Him must have a really nice view of my ass right about now, and I wonder whether he likes it. The way he blocks everyone else's view makes me feel protected, like he wants me and he doesn't like to share.

"Look at me," he orders.

When I do, he's standing above me, with a flock of other men scurrying away. I feel incompetent in his presence—like a total blonde—sitting on my heels and apparently incapable of forming a complete sentence. He serves me a smile and extends a hand in a friendly gesture.

"Can I at least help you up?" he asks, with the most deep and sensual voice.

In a daze I take his hand, gazing into stormy grey eyes with a swirl of darkness. He pulls me to my feet. He's tall—very tall—and clean cut, with dark hair and mysterious eyes.

A girl could get hypnotized by those eyes.

He catches my smile and lets me study him, then with a wink, he plucks me from the dance floor and takes me to the nearest open bar table. He doesn't let me go until I'm being tucked into a seat. I pull my skirt under my thighs and settle onto the chair he offers. He takes the seat across from me and smiles before hollering across the table.

"You okay?"

A nervous laugh reaches my mouth, but I refuse to let it out. "Yeah, I'll be okay." A piece of light brown hair falls into my eyes when I glance down at the table. I brush it aside and fold my lips together.

"I did that once, it doesn't tickle."

My mouth drops open as I take in another look at his striking features. "Tripping in high heels?"

He laughs. "Falling on my ass in public. It's usually a sign of a good time."

I wouldn't know.

"I don't suppose your ass was hanging out, too." I cringe from the memory, even though I still have a bruised knee and a sticky hand as an unwelcome reminder.

"No, I don't think it was. But my ass has had its fair share of public nudity."

I laugh anxiously. *What I would do to see that rock hard ass.*

"Maybe I should save that story for another time," he says, noticing how intrigued I am by his conversation.

I smile softly and nod in agreement as a blush warms my pale cheeks.

"Are you here alone?"

It seems like a bold question, and I should probably lie. "Yeah." I search for something brilliant to add to the conversation. "You?"

His sexy, narrow eyes peek out from beneath the curve of his ball cap. "My brother."

I nod, feeling a little less comfortable in the situation. I wonder if his brother is just as big and beautiful as he is. I sigh, scrunching my eyes to adjust the annoying film over my eyes from the contacts. This guy is tall, dark, handsome, well-dressed—way out of my league. The thought crosses my mind: this is probably only happening because he pities me, because I am here alone.

What was I thinking coming here tonight? I feel like such a fool.

"You look like you could use another drink."

Do I now? Perceptive, he is.

I don't know where I find my nerve, but while I'm here— "Are you buying?" Before I even have a chance to seek out a waitress, one is standing at his side.

"What can I get for you?" She smiles at him seductively.

I could learn a thing or two from this girl. Her shirt is a little tight in the chest; the buttons near her cleavage are busting at the seams. I bet he likes that. But he only looks to me when he speaks.

"Two bottles of Bud, please."

The waitress waits for him to make eye contact with her, but he doesn't. In fact, his eyes never leave mine. He wants to order for me? I'm game, because being under his gaze is a heady cocktail that I'm not ready to give up just yet. I've never reaped this kind of attention from a man before. I must have done *something* right.

"Are you from around here?" he asks me, with a quizzical expression on his face. His voice fluctuates with curiosity and his dark eyes shine with interest. He leans in toward me, and our small table in this crowded room is suddenly feeling very intimate.

"Born and raised, unfortunately. You?"

He shakes his head and takes a long draw from his beer, polishing it off before answering. "Naw. I'm only in town for the weekend. A family thing. But I'd rather not talk about that tonight."

I nod with relief. "I respect that."

A pleasant silence passes between us. I'm all shy smiles and he's all sex-god on steroids. Just sitting at his table has my heart racing and breaths cut short. I've never felt so attracted to a non-fictional man.

"What about you? Let's talk about you," he suggests, being a man of few words.

That makes me super nervous. I never talk about me. I talk about authors and articles and books, but me? No.

"There's nothing much to talk about."

He gets up from his seat and pulls a chair over from the table next to us, stealing it without asking and sliding up beside me until our knees are touching and his arm is hovering behind my back. His fingers skim over my shoulder, tracing the fallen strap of my bra. Everywhere his fingers pass, a wake of tingles follow. Air slips between my lips hurriedly and a coolness creeps along my skin. Nerves. It has to be the nerves.

"I don't believe that for one second. You look like a woman with stories."

The deep seductive sound he makes with his voice is

making it hard for me to breathe. "I do?"

Only one thing is certain: I'm drinking way too fast for a girl who had planned on driving herself home, and yet my beer disappears shortly after it's placed in front of me. I chase it with another Bud. Talking becomes much easier after that. I probably say more than I should, but I'm feeling good—real good—especially when he touches me. And, since I don't expect to do anything like this ever again, I'm going to make the best of it.

It's not until I polish off another bottle of Budweiser that I start to feel the full effects of drinking too much alcohol.

He notices my surprise. "Drink much?"

"Once a year," I admit, then slap my hand over my mouth for giving away how plain and boring my ordinary life is.

Little did I know, that was all about to change.

4

He's Mine

A man waves frantically from across the room, ripping my attention away from the sexy face in front of me. "Uh, I think that guy is trying to get your attention."

Handsome checks to see what I'm talking about and sighs, with an apologetic raise of his eyebrows, just barely flashing me those eyes from under the peak of his ball cap. "Yeah, that's my brother, Rusty. I'll be right back, okay?" He adjusts his hat and leaves me.

Ah, so bulging biceps and good looks runs in the family. Big surprise there. "I'll be here," I say to myself, smiling and wondering where I've found my inner confidence. It doesn't matter if it's only liquid courage. It feels great.

My smile is short lived, as I sip from the bottle of water sitting on the table in front of me, watching a beautiful, leggy blonde with glossy hair and matte lips stalk toward me like she's on a mission. At first I'm worried that I've been hitting on her boyfriend, then I relax back a little. It more looks like she's trying to pick me up by the way she eyes me, like I'm a cherry lollipop and she prefers women.

I figure it out, not a moment too soon. She's actually sizing me up. I get butterflies in my stomach.

"How's it going?" she asks with a breathy seduction.

I'll have to practice that voice!

I glance over each of my shoulders, still wondering if there's someone else behind me who I hadn't noticed before. *Nope. Just me.*

"Me?" I still can't believe this gorgeous woman is talking

to me. She could run circles around me in every way.

She laughs, and the sound sparkles between us. "Yes, you. Who else would I be talking to?"

My cheeks start to warm, but I force through it with a smile. If I'm going to dress the part, then I'll have to play it, too. "Me. Obviously." I roll my eyes, more to myself, but I never roll my eyes. It kind of feels good. I'm tired of being an adult today.

"So, that guy," she starts. "Is he taken?" Her eyes flash across the room.

"What guy?" I ask, following the direction of her heated gaze.

"The sexy one. Ball cap. Mysterious eyes. Hard abs. Nice ass."

"How'd you see his abs?" I say before thinking. Jealousy is not one of my prettiest features.

She laughs again. "He is accounted for then?"

"Did I say that?"

"You didn't have to." She scowls at my face, like it tells her something, so I don't have to. "I knew it." The girl's face falls flat and the strong girl attitude seems to deflate before my very eyes. "There's a terrible drought in this town and I thought I found some fresh meat. Of course he's picked you."

I wave my hand in front of the misery ridden face. "Wait, what?"

She glances across the room again and smiles sadly at him, then looks at me. "You're a striking beauty: bold, and yet innocent. I can't pull that look off at all." She starts to pour her face into her hands, tears literally falling like a raincloud has just hit and let loose over her head.

I'm feeling awfully brazen in this moment, like I've won a small war. "Yeah, I'm pretty lucky. He's amazing." I look up at the man who's the cause of all this commotion and our eyes connect.

Even though I have a girl sobbing into her hands because of me and my one little white lie, I'm smiling like the Cheshire cat. I have to fold my lips over to hide my smile when she looks up at me. Then Mr. Sexy is curling his finger for me to come over to him.

"Sorry, I have to go," I explain, as I fumble to my feet.

Fighting off the giddiness and nerves, I carefully walk across the room, weaving between people with my one target in place. Biting on my bottom lip, I slip up next to my walking wet dream and wait to see what he wants, gaping at how tall and godly he looks.

"What was that all about?" he asks me, smiling, leaning in close so I can hear him better.

Shrugging my shoulders, I feign innocence, soaking up the attention and inhaling his cologne, imagining what it would be like to be tangled up with him for the night.

He smirks. "I'm sorry, what is your name again?"

"Izzabelle," I answer, feeling awfully dumb. We haven't even exchanged names. This feels like a step forward, though, until that dark look falls across his shadowed face. My stomach flip-flops in my throat.

"Are you ball blocking me, Izzabelle?" The way my name rolls off his tongue and the way he licks his teeth after he finishes speaking has my mouth dry, like a desert in a wind storm.

My breaths become labored, but I manage a firm answer, surprising even myself. "Considering that I have no idea what you're talking about, I think I'll go with no."

His laugh is half-hearted. "You know exactly what I'm talking about. I saw that girl approach you. What did she say?"

I lift my nose in my best librarian fashion. "That's not your concern."

"Oh, it is when it has to do with me." His voice rumbles, coming straight from his chest, like a roll of thunder passing between us.

I can't believe this guy, trying to use that sexy voice on me. "How conceited are you? What makes you think it had anything to do with you?"

The look in his eye shows how confident he is. "I saw the way you looked at me."

Shit, fuck. My fingernails urge me to nibble on them and I just barely survive the stare off by gripping onto the hem of my ridiculously short dress with both hands. "What way?"

"The way you are right now: seemingly innocent, with a bad girl hiding beneath just waiting to break through."

I squirm next to him, crossing my ankles and clutching my thighs together. Everything he says is true. I want to feel what it's like to have his lips brush across mine, his tongue down my throat and that hard body flush against me.

His voice booms into my ear when he brings his lips to it. "This virtuous diva act you're putting on for me, like you can do no wrong; I don't buy it—not for a second. You're up to something here and I'm going to find out what."

Is that a threat?

He brushes past me, intentionally bumping into my hip when he does.

What. The. Ever-living. Fuck.

Stunned out of the here and now, I watch him walk toward the teary-eyed girl who's now pouring her heart out to the poor waitress.

The girl!

I shuffle after him. I know he hears me coming, but I don't expect him to turn around. He's smiling—very pleased with himself—when I bump into him. His arms loop around my waist and hold me upright, keeping me pressed into his body.

He licks his bottom lip, which is right at my eye level with these tall shoes on, sending a shiver racking through my entire body. "Don't you worry, Izzabelle. I wasn't going anywhere."

When his thumb brushes down the bared skin on my back, I realize how close I am to having his hands all over me right now.

I want to feel his hands all over me.

Holding his warm, sparkling gaze, he flattens a palm against my back, making for damn sure that I don't leave his arms, or detach from the front of his body. We start moving side to side, like we're dancing to a slow song, my arms sliding around his neck, with the unrelenting pulse between my legs and my breasts crushing against his chest. If we were lying on a bed, we'd be making love.

My sexual appetite hits me like a tidal wave, making urges torture my body unlike ever before. The need to hike up my skirt, wrap my legs around his waist and let him invade me becomes nearly unbearable, with him erect against my stomach. I chew on my bottom lip as he backs me into the wall, and open my mouth to breathe, feeling the strength in his arms.

He makes no move to take my mouth, even with my lips begging him to, my legs becoming weightless with the grip he has on my body. Feeling reckless, I move against him, swaying my hips to taunt him. He growls sensually, his nose coming down to the delicate place behind my ear, his mouth meeting the bare skin of my neck. His lips brush over my shoulder and kiss me there, softly, in stark contrast to the stiffness of every other part of his body.

Sensations saved for a bedroom strike my core and plead with me to go home with him, but a one night stand is a dirty, dirty thing and I am not a bad girl like that. His hands grip onto my hips to stop me from swaying, showing me that maybe I am a little bit naughty, after all. Our eyes meet and exchange a flash of heat. He takes my hips into his hands and twirls me around until I'm facing the wall, backed into him, with his arms hooked around me, an open hand flattened against my stomach and over my breasts. He somehow manages to make this action romantic, molding my body back against his.

He's sweating now, but so am I. I'm not even sure when that happened. I'd like to think that I make him sweat. He smells sweet, his cologne overpowering my nostrils with a fragrance I won't soon forget, as his hands slide down my body to scour me skin-to-skin, like he's worshipping my bare thighs with those rough, masculine hands.

I rock against him, like no one's watching, and rest my head back on his chest, with closed eyes, feeling his rigid body moving against mine in an erotic motion that mimics a sexual act that I'd love to try with him in a more private place. His fingers skip across my skin, feeling every inch of bare flesh like he can't get enough of me. My hair is pulled free from my shoulder and he has to lift up his hat to get a good angle at my neck.

His mouth works magic on my shoulder, with his hands touching me in ways I've never before been touched, let alone in public. With hands slipped under my skirt, he cups my full ass and moves me against him in a way that feels all too wrong, but so very good, making me lose sight of reality. My hands press into the wall for support, with him riding the erratic beat of my heart.

When I flip my hair up, I catch the desire swirling in his eyes, like a hooded veil of need that hadn't been there before. It matches my own. I've never wanted a man the way I want him now. Sex in a public washroom, or a moving taxi-cab, has always seemed so dirty, and just plain wrong to me. I've always told myself that one night stands are for dirty whores, and who knows, maybe they are, but I'm an adult and I choose him, and I refuse to spoil the moment worrying about how many nights our relationship will stand.

I tell you, if he were to pull me to the restrooms right now, I wouldn't be able to say no. The alley out back isn't sounding like such a bad idea right now, either. I just want him. Inside. Outside. *Everywhere.*

He growls in my ear, with his hand smoothing over my inner thigh like he wants more, too.

Yes!

I need him to touch me harder, but when Rusty sidles up next to us, that ends our foreplay. Rusty talks in his ear, while I collect myself, trying for steady breaths, but not getting far. My body screams from the loss of his touch, and I too am afraid my night is over. The look in Sexy's eyes when he takes my hand, to make sure I don't wander too far away, tells me our night has only just begun.

Rusty kisses the girl who's been hanging off him all night while I kept his brother occupied, and tells her he's leaving, without her. My heart races in my chest, like a thousand horses are trampling me and I'm barely surviving, waiting to find out my own demise. Have I read him all wrong?

"Dustin, we have to get out of here!" Rusty shouts, his voice turning into more like a threat than a friendly suggestion.

My eyes catch onto his. "Dustin?"

Dustin smiles into my eyes and cups my cheek, brushing his thumb over the warmness there. "That's my name. I guess I should have told you that sooner."

His thumb passes over the swell of my bottom lip, as Rusty takes off toward the door, leaving us standing there, virtually alone. Although our bodies have become very well acquainted, it is now very apparent to me that he has never touched his lips to mine. Dustin continues to hold my hand in one of his, with an expectant look on his face, his breaths tripping, much like mine.

The depth of his request resonates in my chest. "Are you coming with me?"

My mouth grows dry. *I'd love nothing more!* But I'd be damned if I could admit that out loud. I try to swallow, but it doesn't help, razors seem to have hacked the back of my throat and I can't find my voice. I go for a demure nod, instead. It is in that moment that Dustin leans in to kiss me, pulling off his hat, like he has to claim my mouth this very minute. His lips hover over mine for a breath, and all time stands still.

Fireworks. There's no other way to describe the sensations impaling me when the flesh of those cupid-bow lips meet mine. His lips are soft and wet and forgiving. Although I don't immediately respond, caught up in the way his hand sweeps down my back, his gentle tongue traces the inside of my mouth, something innocent and sweet, taking me to another dimension, stealing my breath and leaving my parted lips much too soon. That one taste is not enough, and my world spins around me in a blur of color.

Dustin takes my hand, holds me close, and practically carries me through the crowd. It feels like I'm flying, soaring above the clouds, with eagerness to see what tonight will bring. He chases down his brother, ignoring the look we get when Rusty realizes they'll have extra company on the ride home. Me.

The warm air bites my cheek when the doorman sets us free. Dustin climbs into the waiting taxi at the curb, and waits for me to join him. When I bend forward to crawl into the backseat, I quickly notice that the car wasn't saved for us. Dustin pats his thigh and, since there's little else I can do, I give him my hand and settle onto his lap.

His hand clasps tighter onto mine, drawing it up his chest, my other hand curling around his neck. Tilting his head toward me, he peers at me from beneath the curved peak of his hat. My eyes collide with his, before fluttering closed. I slant my head sharply to meet his mouth and our lips touch, starting with a soft peck, and another, and another; each kiss growing longer and more fervent. He wraps his lips around mine, seeking entry with his tongue, his hands now framing my face.

Rusty makes a coughing sound right next to us, but neither of us responds. Our kiss only grows more heated and necessary. Dustin is pulling me snugly on top of him, until I'm mounting his hips and his hands are gripping my ass underneath my skirt. The sensation of his hard body grinding against me is enough to make me scream out in pleasure. I whisper in his ear, smiling the entire time, but a moan is inevitable when one of his hands slips between my legs and touches me there.

The rest of the details from this night are a wonderful blur that will wade in and out of my imagination like the tide for a long time to come.

5

Where Am I?

I awaken under a pile of fluffy blankets that secure me to an even fluffier bed. I can't remember the last time I slept in without having to wake to the sound of my alarm clock. Wait a minute. Where am I? With half closed eyes, I stretch my arms out, my fisted hand bumping into a hot slab of flesh. My eyes widen with the realization that there actually is a warm, hard body lying next to me. I try to remember another time that I awoke next to a hulking sex machine like this, but I can't. That would be because this is a first for me.

I gasp for a breath, because it turns out that maybe that crazy, hazy dream I had last night wasn't a dream at all. My eyelashes flutter erratically, my body twisting to see who's lying next to me. The dude is awake. Naked, except for the pale sheet drawn across his one muscular thigh. My eyes don't move any higher than his waist, not even to gawk at the solid collection of abdominal muscles flexing when he turns toward me. With him lying on top of the covers like that, I can see that he is not just awake, but *very* awake.

"Hey you," he growls, in a deep voice that hits me right between the thighs.

Oh shit. Have we done something here? I don't even know.

It'd be a mega shame if I've finally gotten laid after all these years and missed the grand finale with a man built like this. He chuckles when he sees the mixture of emotions playing on my face. I chew on my lower lip, caught between nerves and disappointment. His thumb tugs it free from my teeth and then, holding my chin with that same thumb, he drops an embellished kiss on my lips.

Holy, wow. That mouth on mine does not get old. It's every bit as good as I had dreamed.

When he backs away, he's smiling. "How are you feeling?"

My hand finds my forehead. It's hot and hurts only half as much as my aching muscles and bruised knee. I'm still in one piece, and I'm lying next to him, so I smile hesitantly.

"I didn't catch your address," he continues. "You were pretty drunk. So I half carried you to my place. I helped you use the bathroom, then you passed out."

I'm mortified, and quickly search under the blankets for clothes, feeling rather naked myself. He reads the horror in my expression and doesn't make me ask when I find my dress crumpled around my waist. He covers his lower half with the sheet, thinking that might make me feel a little more comfortable in the situation, but it does little to hide the very erect body part pointing toward me.

I lift the edge of the covers to peek down at how my dress is wrinkled up in a ring around my waist.

"You spilled your drink on your dress, so I folded it down," he says, peering down the covers.

A breath hitches in my throat as I cup my breasts, partly to hide them from him and partly to disguise my embarrassment. "My bra?"

"You took it off in the night. It was see-through anyway."

A part of me wants to die right now. Another part of me squirms about the way he regards my body. One of my hands slides down to my naked thighs.

"My panties?" I cringe as I throw the heavy blankets off of me, leaving us both covered with merely a single thin sheet.

"They were pretty wet, and I didn't think it would be very comfortable for you. I tossed them over there." He points at where my red thong hangs from a small silver handle on the dresser.

"When we were fooling around in the taxi, things got

pretty . . . hot." The way he hesitates on the word hot, like it takes his breath away just thinking about it, has my bared body parts tingling. "You begged me to touch you," he says. "I did. And you were so wet."

That particular body part that I'd finally forgotten about bounces firmly beneath the sheets, attracting my attention. He licks his lips and stares at my mouth, like he wants to kiss me again, touch me. My body throbs with a renewed want for him.

"You didn't seem to mind."

I nod my head slowly, my body lighting up from the memory of his hands touching me in places that haven't been discovered in years. I gulp, noticing that his body starts rising again from beneath the thin sheet next to me.

Squirming in my dress, I smooth it out over my thighs beneath the sheets. Not like it helps much. I'm a train wreck and his healthy, erect body is screaming my name. I have to know. "We didn't—"

"No," he answers, stopping me from saying it. "Not for lack of trying, though."

My eyes bug out of my head.

Oh. My. Word!

"It wasn't you. It was me," he admits. "Too many beers, I guess."

Dustin stretches his muscled body out and the sheet slightly falls over the side of his body again. My eyes zero in on his crotch, like I'm waiting for a lead pipe to spring free.

He chuckles again. "I don't know why you're acting so shy this morning. You were rather engaging last night."

"Engaging?"

He's grinning now, just thinking about it. I wish I knew what has him grinning so hard. "Let's just say you gave me a very creative and helpful hand when we got here. That's probably why I didn't close the deal."

"You mean we were going to—"

He interrupts me again. "I couldn't get it up again. I can't believe you don't remember this. You were pretty disappointed in me. But it was hot and I was drunk as a skunk. So were you, Izzy."

"Izzy? Only my mom calls me that."

"Well, you told me to call you that. I won't anymore, if it bothers you."

I feel like a piece of mortified shit, shaking my head. "It's fine. I'm sorry." I press a hand into my pounding forehead. "I'm sorry for being so rude to you. I'm not usually that . . . outspoken."

I go to turn away, out of embarrassment, but he stops me. His hand cups my cheek, then he leans in close and steals another kiss. It's not a chaste one either. It's long and slow and filled with passion.

I want more.

He pulls away for a breath, and I get my first real look at the pillow beyond his head. It looks strikingly familiar. The matching sheets have a very distinctive design in the one corner, too.

No.

My heart begins to palpitate for a new reason as Dustin leans in for another kiss. The soft lime walls, the white antique dresser, the framed image from my mother's first art class after my dad left us. It's all too much.

"Oh fuck." I push him off of me, frantically. "Where are we?" I ask, but I'm afraid I already know the answer.

"Oh fuck," I say again, frozen in place. "What time is it?"

"About time for me to start getting ready for the wedding, I expect. I crashed at my dad's new place. He's getting married today. Second time's a charm."

"Oh fuck, fuckity, fuck fuck."

I leap out of the bed faster than a flaming race car driver, pull on my panties and yank on the large, white t-shirt lying on the floor. I manage to pry open the door, peer around it, and sneak down the hall and into my old room before Dustin has enough time to pull on his underwear and realize what the hell is going on. The stunned look on his face is priceless. If he thinks that's peculiar . . . *He'll figure it out soon enough.*

6

New Mistakes

In front of my bedroom mirror, I scrub the black makeup out from under my eyes, vigorously blotting my smeared red lips and eye shadow with a tissue. I look like a fucking clown. What was I thinking? The sound of footsteps pounding down the stairs brings me to my feet, my heart racing with curiosity. I pace across the room when I hear the front door slam shut. Is he chasing after me?

I peer out my window and watch Dustin jog down my driveway. Shirtless. A flash of that hard body right next to me crosses over my eyelids. My body vibrates with a remembered desire to have him.

Oh, shit, fuck, shit.

He stops at the end of the driveway and looks both ways, almost frantically, then he sets off toward uptown with a light jog. I watch him until the trees up the road block my view.

How did this happen?

I think back to last night. My memory is awfully foggy, except for a few very vivid images of a very naked, very aroused man lying next to me. Stormy eyes. Naturally tanned skin. Muscles. A man like I've only read about in romance novels. Before now, I didn't believe that kind of man actually existed.

Oh, he does.

I hurry to the bathroom before he returns from his jog, and wrestle with my shower puff to speed through my washing routine. With a towel wrapped under my arms, I sprint to my bedroom, dripping wet. I hear heavy footfalls on the stairs just as my door clicks shut. My heart wins the race, but my lips cannot even smile, a ghostly look washing over my face.

Holy shit. That was close!

Pressed up against the door, a tension wracks my entire body. I close my eyes, where a very erect image greets me, like a daydream. I will never forget the way Dustin held me—felt me—like I was all woman. All *his* woman. My hand slips beneath the oversized bath towel and tickles downward. My fingers press a little harder, to dull the throbbing sensation between my thighs, and then I touch myself.

I don't usually touch myself. I'm more reserved than that. But I need to find relief and this is feeling like a good solution at the moment.

My fingers circle, at first gently and then vigorously, until I drop the towel and slide two fingers inside of me to calm the urge to have Dustin, my *soon-to-be stepbrother*, back in my bed. I hear his voice thundering down the hall. I stiffen instantly, slamming my head against the door. My orgasm takes me away, my body tightening around my own two fingers.

Breaths heave from my chest, like I've just run a marathon, while I stand there frozen in place, temporarily sated. I frenziedly retrieve the towel from my floor, wipe my fingers clean, and shovel it into my basket with the rest of my clothes. I drop backwards onto my bed and my eyes fall shut. It's because I'm frickin' tired, but guess who pops back into my brain already?

I have a feeling that hard body will be the only thing on my mind for a very long time to come. Dustin's hands slide up my soft, bare thighs and cup my ass. Oh, but what if we had—

Knock. Knock. Knock.

My eyes pop open. *Oh, shit!*

"Are you up, honey?" my mom asks sweetly, having no idea about the dirty thoughts running through the head of her seemingly unadulterated daughter.

I jump to my feet and yank on my favorite pair of granny panties. "Yes, Mom. I'll be down in a few minutes." I make the promise softly, cringing the entire time, praying that Dustin doesn't recognize my voice.

That voice. Deep, dark and dangerous, just like our little secret. My fingers press over my white granny panties, to settle the ache reemerging there. I have to shake my head to clear the thoughts and tear my hand away, my permanent headache settling in for the day that will surely be from hell.

7

A Secret

It's almost an hour drive to the Carver Mountain Golf and Country Club, and I have to admit it to my mom. "Jason must really love you to drive this far to work every morning," I say, making no mention of the ruined rose bush on the side of her house.

My mother smiles, so happily. "He really does. Isn't that amazing? Me—lucky enough to find two loves of my life."

"Mom, you never loved Dad. You don't have to say that."

"No! Not your dad. You, sweetheart. You'll always be my first love."

I sigh. That settles it. I have to tell her the truth, no matter how embarrassing. My mom is the sweetest person in the world. I can't lie to her and it's best that it comes from me first. I fiddle with the length of my nude gown. This isn't going to be half as easy as it looks.

"Mom, I have to tell you something, but you're not going to be happy with me." I glance at the beautiful vintage gown she's wearing, happy that she decided to go with a white one even though it's her second marriage. "In fact, I don't think you'll be happy at all."

My eyes reach hers, but she's shaking her head. "Not today, Izzabelle. Nothing can get me out of this beautiful mood. Save it for another day. Can we do that, honey?"

"But—"

"I'm sure it can wait, right?" she insists sweetly.

I was lucky enough that Jason and his boys had taken off

before I made it downstairs. The whole not seeing the bride in her gown on her wedding day thing saved me from a catastrophe—for now—but I'm not quite in the clear just yet.

"Yeah. Of course." I wish it could wait eternally, so I'd never have to tell her, but I've always told my mother everything and I know this isn't something I can keep from her for very long.

Our limousine makes a pit stop at an extravagant little bungalow in the city to pick up the other bridesmaid. It's a pity to waste this huge vehicle on three women, but clearly Jason comes from a family of old money and cost is not an issue when it comes to my mother's happiness.

Jason's sister exits the house, with her bouncy curls and wide smile, matching the charm of her solid, flowery home. She's naturally beautiful. What a surprise. That obviously runs in their family. We're wearing the same dress, but she wears it better. The halter top looks amazing with a bit of breasts to give some shape to the ruched halter top, whereas the gown looks rather flat on me, falling from that ruched sheer fabric into a puddle at my feet.

I wait next to the limousine for my introduction and smile toward them, my mother's voice saving me from having to think of something nice to say. "Izzabelle, this is Katrina, Jason's sister."

Katrina walks toward me with a grace I could only dream of having and reaches out her hand. "Hi, nice to meet you."

I shake the woman's hand. "It's nice to meet you, too. You have a beautiful home."

More smiles. More small talk. Don't get me wrong, the greeting is friendly, but it's awkward, the way they always are for me. I don't find relief again until we're back on the road. Staring out the window, sipping on a cup of water to cure my dry throat, I notice the country club sign first.

Carver Mountain Golf and Country Club.

Jason's country club.

Another sip is necessary to stop me from choking on my

cowardice. The expansive greens are too perfect for words, and the natural trees that gather near the river passing alongside the roadway breathe life into the country. I glance at them hesitantly, like the others will know what I'm thinking about by simply monitoring my eyes.

"Oh wow, Mom. This place is beautiful. I had no idea."

A narrow winding road leads toward the country club and nowhere else. The car turns slowly and time seems to stand still. As the limo pulls up to the front doors of the glamorous building, I suffer from severe spasms in my stomach. I fight to hide it as the stunning sign that announces the special event comes into view. I thought I'd seen enough, but it's not until the limo driver is helping me out of the car that I get my first good glimpse into Dustin's lifestyle.

They must be bathing in wealth. Nice clothes, expensive jewelry, and fast cars. That explains a lot. *Dustin is used to getting what he wants.*

"Jason has taken very good care of this place," my mother explains. "As his father did before him and his oldest will do next."

"His oldest?" I ask, not wanting to hear the answer, but getting it quickly from Katrina.

"Dustin."

I cringe, but quickly practice masking that look.

Dustin.

8

Forbidden

I'm standing at the back of the room, the first woman to set foot in the aisle, so I am the one who gets the collective happy sigh from the shockingly large group of people crowding the aisle. Of course, everyone's looking—and I mean everyone—but I can't tear my eyes away from the two men standing at the halfway mark, in front of their father. The look on Dustin's face when he puts it all together is priceless, much like his brother's. This awkward confession would have to happen silently, as I'm walking down the aisle toward them, with both our families gawking, me walking to the gentle sound of a harp and the men standing there very stiffly in shock.

I ignore my gawking aunt, who's trying to cobble together her own story to explain the looks we're sharing. I can't blame her. It has to be a sight to see. Dustin's jaw practically lands on the floor right next to his brother's tongue, and they don't recover, not even slightly, until I reach for Rusty's arm.

"Shut it," I whisper harshly through clenched teeth in warning, as I take the younger one's elbow and smile for the cameras. I don't care if that wasn't the plan; I make my own rules and I'm not walking the aisle with Dustin. This is embarrassing enough as it is.

My mother doesn't question my reasoning for taking the wrong man's arm, and I try to pass it off like I didn't realize I had.

I swear Dustin's jaw remains slack for the remainder of

the ceremony and well into the reception. Thank God it is all taking place at the same venue. I don't know if I would have survived anything more.

Seated next to my mother at the head table after dinner with a glass of wine held gracefully in my hand, I settle into visions from earlier; the proud stance Dustin exuded, standing next to his father. I don't remember him being so tall. And that hair. The sides are trimmed so neatly, I didn't expect the top to have any length to it, but it does, dark and luscious, making me want to run my fingers through it. I take a long, slow gulp from my glass, finding it empty—again.

I try not to glance at my new family, but hiding from them makes the night drag on, impossibly slow. When the master of ceremonies starts talking, my stomach twists into knots. Shit. It's speech time.

Dustin and Rusty push out their chairs, making them visible to me and to everyone else when they get to their feet in the most handsome of tuxedos. Dustin catches my eye and notices me noticing him but acts unaffected by it all, crossing the front of the room and taking his place next to Rusty at the tall, white podium that's draped in a series of silky fabric. Dustin smiles, but steps aside, leaving the talking to Rusty. I figured as much would happen, Rusty being the more talkative and outgoing of the two, but he rambles and the words start to blend together. My gaze falls to his brother.

My stepbrother.

My eyes travel up Dustin's large, fit body, settling on his broad shoulders and the soft white of his vest. I notice the way his bowtie is tightly wound around his throat and it makes me short of breath. My own body defies me, aches for him, begs for me to find myself in his arms, again. I have to look away to catch a breath that I didn't realize I was holding. A steadying breath is all I take before my eyes flicker back to the podium, warily now. Dustin's just standing there looking sharp with those masculine hands simply resting at his sides, while I get a good, long chance to devour him.

There is no end to the sex appeal of my new brothers. It's unnerving and makes me uncomfortable just sitting in the same room as them. I twist in my seat, remembering how it felt to rub against all that hard muscle, just as Rusty looks to me. All I hear is, "I'm thankful for my beautiful sister, but not half as thankful as Dustin, here."

People laugh. Fuck you, all. This is not funny, not even a little bit. My eyes narrow instantly, to hide the fear pumping through my veins like a poison set to kill. Is this all he's said about me? It had better be. My eyes hook onto his, in warning.

Say it and die, Rusty.

Apparently that isn't the expression people were expecting. I wouldn't know, because my scowl is set on one target. I glare at him, forcing a smile only after my mom's warm hand presses over the back of my own, and I realize that the entire company is staring at us—either him or me. Maintaining my forced smile is difficult when I'm forced to observe the pained look in Dustin's eyes first hand. He turns away, but the fleeting flicker of mischief in Rusty's voice is almost as bad.

The tension fills the space between us, like the pressure from a powerful storm. My ears ring and I don't hear another word that comes out of Rusty's mouth. A breath rushes out of my body when all attention transfers to the happy couple next to me. I pull away from my mother's hand, happily relinquishing the interest of our blended families to her and Jason and their love.

Rusty is lucky he ended it there, too, because I am about to pass out. Even with Dustin across the room, it feels like he has invaded my space, the migraine that had plagued me earlier returning with a vengeance. I can feel the eyes of two men on me. They want everyone to believe it's my mother they're smiling at, but I know better. My eyes flicker next to me, to see what's got everyone's panties in a bunch.

One thing is for certain: my mother is happy. I swallow and smile awkwardly when Jason kisses her. Everyone starts clapping. I assume the speeches are over.

Thank God! I need to get out of here.

My chair slams backwards, but I crash into something hard. I catch Dustin's eye when his hand graces my naked shoulder, and I take a shuddering breath. Electricity crackles in the air between us, and time freezes in place, until I tear my gaze away. Suddenly, leaving the table is not an option. If I get to my feet now, I will surely fall. I huff, tugging my chair back in, until I'm tucked back under the table, mumbling an apology.

He smirks and takes his seat down the head table, next to his father. I refill my glass, tip it up and gulp it back. My cheeks warm, and the empty glass of wine in front of me is of no help.

"Slow down, sweetie," my mom says, smirking at me.

I smile back at her, refilling my glass with a shaky hand. "I can handle it, Mom."

At least my mother blocks the space between me and that dangerous slab of rock. It's bad enough that he'll be keeping me up tonight with dirty thoughts of what could have been, I don't need to see that handsome face again. She and Jason sit there, with their hips latched together like smiling Siamese twins, like a stone wall put in place specifically to keep Dustin and I apart. It's been an effective deterrent for the majority of the night, but it's now time for the happy couple to share the first dance.

They stand, leaving the chairs between Dustin and I very empty. I focus on my mother and smile. She really is happy. I'd almost forgotten to enjoy it for her. It's hard to stay fixated on contentment, though, with the reminder of what I have to do next. After the first minute of the song, I'm to join in with my new brother—the oldest one, the taller of the two. Yeah, I don't think so. Although my mother was rather specific, so I don't make the same mistake twice, that's exactly what I'm trying to do.

When I casually glance next to me, I notice that I'm the only one now sitting at the table. Everyone's paying attention to the dance floor, even the wedding party, so there's no need for me to feel embarrassed. Other guests are getting up, framing the dance floor on foot, while I frantically search heads for my dance partner.

Do you realize how small our wedding party is? Let's just say, my selection of dance partners is limited. I've managed to steer clear of Dustin so far, and made friends with a couple bottles of bubbly instead. If I've made it this far, I think I can survive a dance. I just need to find a safe partner. I try to search for Rusty, but notice my smiling mother in the process. Her vintage dress sweeps the floor, like she and Jason are dancing on clouds, and the happy couple shares a kiss. Everyone awwws and it stops even me in my tracks.

Yeah, I can see. They're so cute. Let's rub it in my face a little harder. I flash a glance toward the man in black—Rusty!—but when I reach out for him, he dodges me and steals my mother away from Jason, swinging himself into the spotlight. I dig my heels into the floor, while others delight in Rusty's move.

You have got to be kidding me!

Jason accepts his sister's offer to dance before I can intervene, which leaves me with only one other option, if I'm to keep to my mother's rules: *Dustin.*

Standing at the opposite end of the dance floor is a tall, handsome man dressed in black. My searching gaze lands on his feet, slowly moving up his body until our eyes clash. I draw a long breath, pulling courage into my lungs, so I don't crumble to the floor and cower from the unrealistic responsibility placed upon me. We stare at each other, my heart tumbling in my chest, his on his sleeve. Now is the time that I must prevail. I can't let fear rule my life.

I swallow, watching his lips wrap around that fat cigar, a phantom mouth moving across my bare skin. It's like he's blowing that smoke along my naked body, where it barely curls between his lips, his eyes trained on me the entire time. My teeth dig into my bottom lip, despite my best efforts to remain unaffected by him. He knows exactly what he's doing to me. *Damn him!*

I can't look away, but neither does he. I don't dare move,

not wanting to break the intensity linking us together like a tightly pulled string. He doesn't think anything has changed between us. If the reins are off then why are his feet glued in place? It's like my heels, too, have sunk into the cement and they've dried there. It takes an oblivious dancing couple to swirl between us to break the strength of our connection. Knowing how ridiculous we both must look, I take the first step toward him. Someone has to. He starts to move in my direction, too, until we meet at the center of the dance floor, staring into each other's eyes.

With the cigar clenched between his teeth, he lifts a hand and I swallow as he enfolds it around mine. I timidly rest my wrist on his opposite shoulder, careful to keep a draft of smoky air between us. One of his hands gently cups my waist; an act of a gentleman. Still, the potency of being this close to such a masculine influence makes me glance away to gasp for a breath. I do not want him to know how he makes me feel. *It ain't even right!*

I smile at my mom, finally hearing the lyrics to the song, as Jason steals the cigar from Dustin's mouth jubilantly and rejoins his life partner. They've truly found the love of their lives, it's plain for all to see, and it tears me apart, not because I don't want that for them, but because that leaves me to be just me.

The song is an emotional one, about losing hope and finding love, and like every wedding song, it makes tears form in the corners of the eyes of the listeners—mine included. Dustin snares my thoughtful gaze, but doesn't say a word to me. He couldn't possibly know there's no saving me, but he wipes the tears away before they roll down my cheeks. Now that his mouth is free of the cigar, I'm holding my breath. To see those cupid-bow lips so closely, when I thought I'd never find myself in his arms again, is terrifying. It only tightens the sexual tension between us.

His hand grips onto my waist, drawing my alarmed eyes to his. Even as other guests join us on the dance floor, it feels like it's only him and me, our feet slipping over the smooth, shiny surface. The more we dance, the farther separated from our immediate family we become. Is this on purpose? I don't imagine it is, but Dustin pulls me a little closer, silently suggesting that it is.

Our bodies press together, him wrapping both of his arms around me, while searching my eyes. His breath is sweet and rich. I inhale it deeply, loving the dark flavor, while mourning the loss of his closeness before it's even broken. Dustin licks his lips, and I look up at him through glassy eyes, with the sting of guilt blazing strong in my heart. I fear the act of wiping away a tear for what I might find in his wild eyes when I can see clearly again.

I plead with him, selfishly, without saying a word. We must maintain the conspiracy of silence. This can't happen. My mind screams—*Please don't!*—while my body screams—*Please, yes!*—greedily. I'm afraid our body language alone will tell the entire story to any family paying close attention. My lips beg for his to come down on mine, while I fight with the drunken urge to announce to everyone what I have done.

It's like Dustin knows what's plaguing me and pulls me from the dance floor before the song is even finished. I scoop a glass of white wine off a proffered tray as we pass a waiter near the exit leading outdoors. My skirt swishes between my legs, making it difficult to walk quickly, but Dustin doesn't slow down. I try to sip from my crystal glass, making wine dribble all down my chin. He pulls me through the ivy covered arbor, and beyond the pool house, where the sky is dark and the stars hover above us sparkling brightly. It's stunning, the beauty of the night unreal.

Dustin releases my hand when I try to stop, and continues walking.

I devour his backside, fascinated by his natural charm. "I think we've gone far enough."

"You think?" His voice mocks me, the first words we've shared since early this morning. Still, he doesn't look at me.

I huff at him, the wine having long ago kicked in. "I didn't know, okay? How the hell was I supposed to know who you were?" I take another gulp from my glass, like it's my lifeline.

Dustin shakes his head, his eyes finally meeting mine. I see the war waging in his stormy eyes. He pulls at his hair with both hands, stepping away from me, but then pacing back. "Thank God I had whiskey dick or we might have actually—" I wait for him to say it, with wide eyes, but he only adds, "You know."

Yes, I do know. The delightful thought makes my stomach flip-flop, and not in a brother-sister kind of way. "That would have been bad."

"Very bad," he adds sharply.

His insistence hurts my feelings. I'd thought his intentions were clear, but obviously I have read him all wrong. I accept his wayward glance with a wobbly lower lip.

"I wonder what excuse I'll use for tonight," he says, tearing my theory to shreds. His eyes land on my lips.

I force them to remain still, my voice a soft breath in the night. "Tonight?"

The silence hangs in the air between us for only a moment before he tugs me against him, sending what's left of my wine spilling to the ground and my glass shattering against the stone building next to us. I grab ahold of the satin-trimmed lapels of his tuxedo jacket to hang on as his lips come down on top of mine.

My body burns for him—for more—but I can't. It's not right for me, for him, and for my mother's sake I have to do this. I drag my mouth free from his, my hands gripping his jacket fiercely, but he still hovers very close to my lips, both of us knowing exactly why I've pulled away and neither of us wanting to let go just yet.

"We can't do this," I say, with half-opened eyes. My sigh can be heard from the far end of the yard as he lifts me upright. I refuse to admit that he's the reason I'm weak in the knees, but I'm also glad that he doesn't let me go completely.

"What's done is done," he says.

I nod, because I agree. "It was all honest. I can't regret

that. I had a *good* time."

"*Good*? Need I remind you how *good* of a time you had?" What starts as a shout that echoes across the yard, turns into an uncanny whisper that licks across every inch of my bare skin.

I want him.

I want him so bad I can feel it in my bones.

I can't have him.

I can't.

9

Unwanted Memories

Every time I close my eyes, even with him standing before me, I'm pulled into unwanted memories of Dustin—his hands clinging to my hips, his mouth hovering over my belly. His tongue—

Yeah.

My eyes blast open to catch his molten hot gaze enjoying every moment of discomfort he gives me. For the first time in my life, I feel filthy hot—and not in a bad way. I feel things I've only read about in the dirty romance novels I enjoy so much, and I don't want this experience to end, but this ain't no fairytale where the couple lives happily ever after in holy sanctuary.

I would burn in hell.

He would burn in hell.

Our sex life would belong in a fiery hell, for sure.

"You want to be with me," he states. It's not a question, and he would be right.

I shrug my shoulders, indifferently. "I did, last night. But that was before I knew we were becoming family." My nipples harden in my dress as the fabric brushes across them. It's as if my body hadn't heard my dilemma and continues to burn for him.

Dustin loosens his grip on me and a flicker of anger flashes in his eyes. "What's that even matter to you? You know now."

I let him loose and break free from his clutches. Maybe if I put a little distance between us, I can think more clearly.

My heels sink into the moist grass as I step away from him. I try to think, but I can still smell him. His cologne, mingling with cigar smoke. His anger. His *desire*.

Spinning around I narrow my gaze. I have to set things right, and I can't show any sign of weakness. "Face it. We will never be able to reconcile our differences. You're my brother now. Clearly we were doomed from the start."

"It's not that easy," he points out, with a smug look on his face. "And I'm not your brother."

I sigh with a long, harsh breath, fighting off the shiver wracking my body from that single, frank statement. "Look. Although the events from last night are still a little foggy, I think I can leave tonight with my dignity intact. This can't happen. I don't fault you for trying, but you're fighting a losing battle."

I realize now that I've had more than my fair share of wine and it's giving me loud, loose lips. Whenever I drink, I tend to ramble. Dustin doesn't stop me.

"I didn't know who you were. It's a trying time for us both, and forgive me for looking for a little comfort. It was nothing we can't forget ever happened."

The passionate snarl on his face tells me that he feels otherwise.

But, why does he have to look that damn sexily at me?

He pauses, staring at my mouth, and licks his lips. "So, that's it?" He asks this unsmiling.

My body screams—No!—but I fight the attraction off so I can be smart about this. "I'm a by-the-book kind of girl, in case you didn't notice that in the whole twenty four hours we've known each other."

He pounds a sarcastic fist into his chest, like I've stabbed him and left the blade hanging there, after twisting the hilt. He mocks me, like he's ill-mannered, when I know he's not, but I guess he does have a point. I haven't even given him a chance, but how could he possibly know anything about me? Sure, my mom's talked about him and Rusty, casually, but I doubt Jason's spoken a word of me. Men don't talk about that kind of thing with their sons. Do they?

I ignore that and finish what I've set out to say. No more procrastinating. "I don't make exceptions and I certainly don't accept excuses. I'm sure our parents would agree that what we're doing is wrong."

Dustin nods at me, but I know it in my heart that he doesn't agree. I just do. That should scare me, repulse me. So, why do I feel it in every fiber of my being that I need this right now? I need him.

"Hey, all we're doing is talking," Dustin says, although I remember quite distinctly what it felt like when he had his mouth on me, not very long ago. His smile turns dangerously sexy, noticing my silent observation.

This is bad.

Bad. Bad. Bad.

He takes a step toward me. I take one step backwards. His next step is larger and I now realize that there's no way my little legs can save me now, digging into the soft grass. I go to make a run for it anyway, twisting my ankle in the process, landing in a heap of nude silk and organza, with a squeak that echoes through the magically vacant night.

Dustin collects me in his arms. Dropped to his knees, he still looks wildly dangerous, the storm in his eyes threatening me as much as that menacing voice. "There's nowhere to run."

His threat has my body humming with a yearning that won't go away until we take care of some unfinished business. I look up into that sinister storm, his eyes saying so much without saying anything at all. All I know is, if his body can match what his eyes are doing to me, I'm in big trouble. He accepts that challenge, leans in slowly, his eyes falling shut, until we're connected at the lips.

"This," he says. "This is why we need to be together." He kisses me again, tugging on my lower lip like an animal, less playful and more daring. The warmth of his body spreads through me, driving away the chill of the night.

I don't push him off, not even when his warm breath rushes over my lips and his body grinds into mine. I sink into his arms and kiss him back, matching his fervor, allowing him to slip his tongue into my mouth and his right hand beneath my now-soiled dress.

"Tell me you remember how explosive we are together." He doesn't stop kissing me, like a volatile creature unable to control itself. His hand slides up the length of my calf slowly, then over the curve of my thigh, sparking the nerve endings to life. "You said things are a little foggy. I want to remind you what you missed out on." His lips travel down my neck, across my shoulder, grazing along all the soft spots exposed to him.

"Wait," I gasp, but the lust in my voice is all the answer he needs to ignore my request.

"Do you remember the way I touched you?" His fingers skim up and around to my inner thigh.

I nearly expire. My mouth drops open and I pant softly. He watches every reaction, calculating his next move from my responses. There's no more fighting him.

He wins.

You win.

I'm nearly in tears, waiting for him to touch me—I mean, really touch me—but Dustin takes his time. Kisses rain down upon me, sliding across my upturned throat, to that place behind my ear that he found the other night, all the way back down to my collarbone. The coolness of his skin passing across my overheated flesh makes me clutch onto him like it's nobody's business. He knows that he's won. He's taking his time, and I have become his outlet. I am his to do with as he pleases.

"Do you remember how I touched you?" He actually expects an answer this time.

"Yes," I breathe, but I'm not answering his question. I like the direction he's going as he presses his hardened body against me.

"I touched you like this." His fingers slide between my legs and touch me where he's left me tingling and wet, but that's not enough. Soon he's pulling my underwear aside, my legs involuntarily spreading wider, making him moan as his fingers sink inside of me. The slow and steady assault has me squirming against him and pleading softly for reprieve. *I need more.*

He knows that look. He knows he's tortured me enough, or so I thought before he pulled his hand free of my layered skirt. Then he makes sure I'm watching, my body shuddering as he slips his fingers between his lips and sucks them clean. He acts like my body is a treat, something highly cherished, his tongue licking over his fingers, looking me right in the eye as he smacks his lips together. "My favorite flavor."

My heart is pounding so hard that I think it might burst from my chest. My body convulses when a breeze slips up my skirt, making me squeeze my thighs together. Dustin gently massages the goosebumps on my legs until they disappear, just for another group of bumps to form from the way he touches me.

"This isn't going to do," he says into the wind, flattening my dress over my lap and pulling me to my feet.

I feel unraveled in his charge, and then he kisses me, with his hands clutching my hips and his wet lips caressing my soul. If he were to push me up against the trunk of a tree and deprive me of my innocence, I would let him, without resistance. He loves being the one in command, and with every touch, I lose a little bit of myself to him.

Gathering my long curls in his splayed fingers, he explores my mouth with his tongue. I feel ravished in the best possible way, with swollen lips and flushed cheeks, and a tension building in my womb. He hovers over my mouth, like he has something to say, but doesn't want to stop and ruin the moment.

"Maybe we should go somewhere," he breathes, his warm breath rushing over my cheek.

The second he witnesses my nod, he dashes around the corner of the building and carefully searches the yard before rushing the maintenance door of the pool house without ever releasing my hand. I notice the door is covered with ivy and hidden by trees but he knows right where to go, the master key sliding into the lock, a perfect fit, like my hand in his.

He pulls me inside, tugs me up a narrow staircase to the second floor, and through a door held ajar to a small room with a day bed in the corner. There's a pedestal sink along the wall, and a toilet with the lid up. It's dark—really dark—except for the faint light from the moon spilling in a dusty window, and yet I can still tell quite clearly that the room is for men only. Simple. Masculine. Uncomplicated.

"It's not much," Dustin says, sounding like he's second-guessing bringing me up here. He walks across the room and twists the knob on a dusty, old lamp, light flickering from the lampshade and casting shapeless shadows across the ceiling. The fact that he believes this man cave would scare me away brings a smile to my face. He licks his lips, watching the way I regard him, knowing now that nothing will override my desire in this moment.

He steps forward and pulls me flush against him, my body responding to every touch, a moan slipping from my lips. I step backwards with him, into the darkness, seeking a wall, but my calves bump into something solid. I drop backward, until I'm sprawled out on a small, single bed, no larger than a fold-away cot.

Dustin watches over me, a haunting, dark figure, as he shrugs off his single-breasted jacket and tosses it aside. His fingers deftly untie his bow, leaving it loose around his neck. He moves to the buttons on his vest, his fingers sliding up to the neck of his shirt, all the way down to his muscled waist, until all that white flags at the sides of his magnificent body. This man is perfection. The rigidness of his abs matches every other muscle on his body, and it's all mine—at least for tonight. I'll worry about tomorrow another day.

He climbs on top of me and I come up to meet him, our lips crashing together, tongues tangling, body parts clashing. He gives off the impression that he's bad as he unties my top and pulls on my dress to expose my breasts, but soon his hands are in my hair, like he cherishes every moment we spend together. He's a mystifying blend of sweet and wicked that I must explore further. Harder. Faster.

Forgetting how small the bed is, getting caught up in the moment, Dustin rolls under me, sending us tumbling onto the hardwood floor in a tangle of limbs and lips. I can't help but giggle, and his smile gets me right in the gut. He catches my chin and gives it a wet kiss. We both know what we're doing right now is forbidden, and yet neither of us speaks of it. Instead, I crawl on top of him, knowing what I'm going to get when I ask for it. I drag my mouth away from his kiss, my breaths coming heavily now.

"Are you sure this is what you want?" I reach for the fly of his pants, chewing on my lip, knowing he does, so much.

His hand is cupped firmly at the juncture between my thighs, where he found me slick with excitement. He slides his middle finger over me, a sensual touch barely hampered by the wet fabric of my panties, pulling his hand away only to graze himself against me. "I need this like the greens of my golf course need sunlight."

There's a serious look in his face as he gazes into my eyes, waiting for me to do as I bid. "What about you?" he asks. "Is this what you want?"

Silly question at a time like this, but if he needs to hear it, I'll tell him.

"If we're just talking about what I want right now, then yeah, this is it." I pull him out of his unzipped pants, with the most beautiful piece of man clutched in my hand. He's long and smooth and perfect. I can see, as my small hand twists up and around him, that Dustin can't take much more of it. He shudders beneath my fingers. What a powerful display of desire. I smile softly, but he turns that gentle threat around on me, flattening me on the warm floorboards.

I hold onto his thick arms, as he rips my panties aside, and thrusts inside of me, grabbing onto my hips and driving himself deeply. I cry out in ecstasy, knowing damn well that someone might hear, but not much caring anymore. My cries only encourage him to press harder.

It takes a few seconds for my body to welcome him and, after a long, hard stroke, he slows his stride, leaning up so he's resting on his forearms. His mellow gaze sinks deep into mine, his silken body sliding even deeper inside me.

I gasp as his fingers press into my pursed lips to hush me. "Shhh." His body tightens when he's forced to support his weight on one arm. I feel that delicious tension everywhere, my coiled body waiting for its release, like a held breath waiting for permission to resume.

Dustin feels it too, squeezing his eyes shut like he's in pain, reaching out for something to hang onto, and clinging onto the metal bedpost with one hand over my head.

"God damn, woman, this feels good."

I wrap my legs around his hips and he digs my lower back into the hard floor. I groan, torn between a sweet pain and delirious pleasure. Slipping my arms around his hot body, I lift myself up until we're rocking back and forth, pressed together like we're one. I draw my chin over his shoulder and dig my nails into his strong back beneath his open shirt, hanging on for the ride, taking him deeper and deeper with every jolt of his hips.

"Oh, God," I shout, breathlessly. "I'm going to finish."

I've never felt pleasure quite like this, and I've never experienced an orgasm sitting up before. I start to counter his thrusts, excited by the notion, riding him like he's a wild stallion and I want him to run faster.

"Wait," he says. "You have to stop."

"No!" I cry, forcing him to go faster and harder.

"Izzy, I'm not wearing a condom," he whispers, like a warning he doesn't want me to heed. "I'm going to finish inside you if you don't stop."

That makes my insides tighten around him and my head flies back. I shout his name as my desire unfurls around him, and I grip the floor behind me, my nails like claws digging into the wooden floor beneath us. He knows now that I don't want him to stop, so he doesn't, thrust after thrust, driving me deeper and deeper into that dark pool of need. He knows how wrong taking me this way is, but I don't stop him, and it only makes it that much more gratifying.

"Yes!" I cry out to the ceiling, like a prayer, loving how hard he takes me. With my breasts bouncing, my body spirals out of control, and he conquers me with one final plunge.

Dustin seizes, in an unnatural pose, with a masculine groan that sends me into an unworldly frisson of awareness. With his muscles all held taught and his chest heaving, he takes my mouth, dominating my body and mind, stealing my breath and my heart.

A fist on the door downstairs puts an end to our resultant kiss.

Bang. Bang. Bang.

"Dustin, that's quite enough!" a man hollers from the bottom of the steps. "Keep it down up there. Your grandmother can hear you, for God's sake." Jason stumbles on his words, while we're both plastered together with sweat and shame and exhilaration.

Dustin smirks first. We haven't been discovered just yet. Neither of us heard my name in the mix. He gives me a swift kiss and pulls free from my body. Crouched on all fours, my eyes catch the flatness of his stomach and lower to study all his masculine glory, which happens to have remained rather erect, even after such a wondrous finish.

"Keep looking at me like that and I'll give my dad another reason to bother us," he growls.

I scowl at him, but refuse to speak. I'm enraptured by the euphoric experience, but terrified of getting caught, maybe even a little ashamed, as my senses start to return to me. That last thought leaves my belly twitching with anxiety. I adjust my dress so everything's as it should be. I tousle my hair, but it's no use. The *just fucked* look is all I have to go with at this point.

Cleaning myself up, I huff when I think of what my mother would say if she found out it was me with Dustin. "I have to go and be seen," I say softly, waiting patiently for a response, but Dustin doesn't saying anything. Something in me snaps, and I'm suddenly angered by his calmness. "Without you."

That gets his attention, but only for a moment. Redressed, he takes a seat on the bed and lies back, nonchalantly, like he's not in any hurry to get out of here. "Do whatever you have to do," he finally says.

There's no kiss goodbye, no thank you very much, no nothing. I huff again, rather than unravelling into an alcohol-enhanced rage, while glancing out the small, dirty window. I wait for Jason to reenter through the back patio doors, then hike up my skirt and rush toward the door, not sparing another glance at Dustin for fear of what I might find.

"Whatever, I'm going," I say, rushing through the door and down the stairs, stopping only to peer through another small window in the door, to make sure no one notices my exit. I just might get out of this one unscathed.

If life were only that simple.

10

Turn It On

I've already made my rounds by the time Dustin appears at the far end of the room with a girl on his arm, his bowtie back in its formal knot. He snares my gaze, but instantly releases it. My stomach catches in my throat, together with my last breath. I watch, like a scorned ex, studying his every move, obsessing over the way he gathers the girl in his arms for a dance, the way his lips quirk upward when she speaks to him. That one small act has my heart tripping.

Stop it, Izzy. Jealousy doesn't become you. He's not yours to obsess over. You said so yourself, he'll never truly be yours.

With a deep breath, I turn on a smile and act like I'm listening to my relatives standing with me, nodding when they speak, replying when necessary, all the while being careful to avoid a certain corner in the room. I know his body moves across the floor, gracefully, like a dark shadow trying to take me over to the dark side. That's it. Time to stop it. No more thinking about *him*. I will not allow this man to ruin my night more than he already has.

My eyes flick to the live band instead, which is actually playing the classics quite well, but the wine in my glass is disappearing faster than it should and the bottle is soon empty, making me look around with a narrowed eye to see who's been sneaking drinks from it.

"Slow down, Izzabelle," my mom tells me, smiling. "Aren't you having a good time?" She squeezes both my shoulders, noticing the way emotion tickles the corners of my eyes, while I swirl what's left of the wine in my glass.

"Mmm hmm," I slur, before taking a long, healthy swallow. "This wine is just really good."

My mom doesn't buy it, and proves that by stealing my wine glass and then kicking her sparkly silver sandals off. She slips her hand into mine and regards me cheerily. "Come!"

I'm pulled to the center of the dance floor in front of the live band, where lights are flashing, tearing me from any sense of reality. Somewhere in that dark, sparkling room I lose myself to the moment. The music is blaring, a feel good song that threatens to steal me away, but my mom hangs on to one of my hands, keeping me grounded.

"Are you ready?" she asks, with a cheeky grin, before spinning me around like she did when I was a child, dancing to the old style of rock and roll.

For once, my smile is not forced. Skipping around like a child with my mom is actually turning out to be quite fun. To avoid a twisted ankle, I pull off my soiled heels, toss them under a table, and return to my mom. Once the guests notice how the bride is having such a good time, others start to join us. Cameras start flashing and I don't even know what's happening until I'm sitting flat on my ass, on the floor, with a huge smile on my face.

"Oh!" my mother shouts, dropping onto the floor next to me. "Are you okay?" She's snickering the entire time, and the camera lights keep flashing.

"Stop laughing at me, Mom!" I say playfully. When she doesn't let up, I warn her again to stop laughing. "Mom!"

She's ear-to-ear smiles, and I can't help but feed off her giddiness. I smile at her squatting there, with her vintage evening gown puddling next to me on the floor. I second guess what I'm about to do, only for a moment, deciding to go for it anyway. I attack her to the floor with a hug. In her ear, I say, "I'm so glad you're happy, Mom. Jason's a good guy. I'm glad you found him."

She clings onto me, not caring that I've probably ruined her expensive dress, and presses a kiss into my warm cheek. "Me too, honey. Me too."

Jason's the one to come to my mom's rescue, prying me off of her, helping me to my feet first, before collecting her in his arms. He steals her away, flashing me a friendly smile, and I return it, but it slowly fades, as I realize how long it's been since I last saw my new stepbrother. The dull ache in my stomach turns swiftly into a screaming warning. I rush to the washroom, like my hair is on fire, and empty a night's supply of wine into the toilet. I dare not look at myself in the mirror, even as I gargle water and spit it out. What is going on with me?

Holding my full skirt in a bunch at my side, I leave the washroom to locate my shoes. When I finally find them under a table, I don't bother putting them on. Ignoring the smiling guests, I head for the smaller of the two balconies, in need of a good breath of fresh air, but not before plucking another bottle of wine from an empty table. It's half gone, but I don't even care, hoping only to drown myself into subservience.

The tiled floors are cold on my feet when I step over the threshold taking me outside, but the coolness of the night is refreshing. The balcony looks like an extension of the ballroom, with oversized floor tiles and lavish furnishings. My eyes lift to find a man standing at the edge of the balcony, looking out beyond the glass railing.

The night is dark, the patio is dimly lit, romantic, and we are the only two in the outdoor room. The man glances over his shoulder and smiles at me cautiously. I let out a relieved sigh, not sure how I would have reacted if he was who I thought he was. It's only Rusty.

It's only Rusty.

But he continues to stare at me, in a way that sends a prickling sensation down my bare back. "What?" I say, but even that single word comes out as a slur.

He moves swiftly toward me, and when I stumble over my own two feet, wine splashing from the bottle in my hand, he catches me. This time, when he smiles, it's for real.

"Funny how you saved that bottle, when you had to choose between it and your face." He smirks at me, the only reason I'm on my feet being his sturdy arms and strong back.

"Well, thank *you* for choosing my face." I stop talking when I realize how ridiculous I'm behaving. A softness plagues my body, my legs feeling much like Jell-O. Rusty holds his hands out a few inches away from me, like I might fall if he doesn't hang on.

"Ha ha," I mock, handing him the bottle of wine, since I'm singularly responsible for the drought in this place.

I thought he was seizing the bottle in order to chastise me, but he takes a long, steady draw from it, suggesting that maybe I'm not the only one with issues tonight. Glancing out over the greens with me, our blurry eyes matching, Rusty sighs. "Damn weddings. Always depressing the single guys."

"You're depressed?" I ask, like I find it hard to believe, because I do.

"And you're not?"

"Okay, okay. I call a truce." After a couple of back steps, I plop down onto the extravagant patio furniture. I note that it's more comfortable than every chair in my townhouse before pointing at the bottle in Rusty's hand. "Give me that."

Rusty smirks and moseys forward, taking a seat next to me. I rip the bottle of wine from his hand and down another gulp, hugging the bottle like it's my lifeline.

"What's got you all worked up tonight?" he asks.

"How do you know I don't act like this every night?" I turn away to stare into the ballroom, through the patio doors, where I see Dustin still has company. I quickly look away, but Rusty's already noticed my problem. Am I that transparent? Obviously!

"I see." He hesitates, likely because he knows better than to talk to me about this, but he says it anyway. "Don't take this the wrong way, but you're not his type."

"Excuse me?" Even if I am half the woman I want to be, I still take offense, making me officially downright mad.

"He always goes for the tall, confident blondes. You're a little on the sweet side, and maybe too reserved. Not that my brother isn't, but opposites attract." Rusty nods toward his brother, who's chatting up the skinniest bitch in the place with icy blonde hair and perfect tits.

"They're probably fake," I say, making Rusty burst into laughter.

He smirks at me, with his arm resting on the sofa behind my back, like maybe we can be friends. "Yeah, my thoughts exactly." Then he adds, "Not that I'm complaining."

I roll my eyes at that. What a surprise that he's not such a bad guy, but he also happens to like plastic tits. I smack at him, like a sister would swat her kid brother for being smart-mouthed. He lifts his knee in defense and outright laughs this time.

"Hey, you're not so bad," he admits, his mood somber, like mine.

I sigh as I lean forward to lose the bottle of wine on the coffee table. My head is pounding, and my world is spinning on a tilted axis. I really shouldn't drink like this; my body isn't used to it and my mouth doesn't know how to react anymore.

"Weren't you wearing lipstick earlier?"

I squint at Rusty, wondering what he's getting at. He leans toward me and runs his thumb over my bottom lip, and at first I think he's flirting with me, but it doesn't seem sexual in any way. Then it hits me. With wide, horrified eyes, my jaw drops open. He shows me his thumb. It's clean—like, completely lipstick-free. Cringing in my own personal hell, he tells me, in not so many words, that he knows I've been making out with Dustin out back. How was I to know my lipstick is smudged across my face and wiped clean off my lips?

Moaning my embarrassment only makes it echo across the room. I don't want to be here anymore. Rotating my body away from the ballroom, I lean over and rest my head on Rusty's shoulder, lifting my aching feet onto the cushion next to me.

"Is this okay?" I ask. It feels like a comfy spot, but the last thing I need to do is offend my new brother.

His left arm curls around me and in turn, he sighs, resting the side of his head against mine.

"Well, don't you two look cozy," a deep voice booms from the doorway, tearing my gaze from the floor.

Dustin's still got the blonde bimbo on his arm, so I try to pay him no attention and go back to resting my eyes, with my cheek against Rusty's chest. Dustin moves farther into the room, leaving the girl at the door, but she shuffles after him, stopping directly across from me, so I can't open my eyes without seeing them both. It's hard to act unaffected by his explicit disregard for my feelings, but I manage, with the strength in Rusty's cynicism pushing me along.

"What do you think you're doing?" Dustin's sharp in his tone, as unpleasant as it gets.

"Fuck off, Dustin," Rusty barks back. "We're tired."

I just barely fight off the smile, gazing into Rusty's eyes up close, while wondering if this is making Dustin jealous. I will not let him ruffle my feathers.

"I don't even know why you thought you liked him," he says to me, kissing me softly on my forehead.

"It's okay," I answer, making for damn sure Dustin knows how I feel about his betrayal. "Lucky for me, most pencils have erasers." My eyes drill into his, narrowed and filled with hatred, anger disguising my fear while he tries to intimidate me with those dark, seductive eyes.

"I don't believe, not for one second, that you can erase me from your memory."

He's probably right, but I refuse to let him continue to believe that. "Why don't you leave us alone?"

"Yeah," Rusty agrees. "You look like you've got your hands full." His reference to the girl's oversized breasts makes me snicker, especially when she lifts her chest to accept the comment for what it is. "And you look like a fool with that lipstick all over your face."

My lipstick!

My soft snicker turns into a slightly louder giggle that erupts into full blown laughter. Suddenly Rusty's laughing, too, but it looks like we're the only two who get the joke.

Dustin and the blonde stand there like we've grown an extra head, and that's okay with me. I needed the laugh, and I want to piss Dustin off. Oh, and it's working brilliantly.

The way Dustin scowls at Rusty, I know he's not at all impressed by our friendship. *Jealous, are we?* He scowls at me next, as his lovely guest tugs on his arm and manages to pull him toward the door. He resists at first, but then he gives in to her. I watch him walk away, wiping at his face. With a smirk on my face, I shoot him the finger, still laughing it up with Rusty, because if I didn't laugh, I'd cry.

Izzabelle is alone again, not literally, of course, but alone in this world. What a surprise that I find myself this way. Had I hoped for more? I was stupid to believe I might actually get to have my cake and eat it too. That kind of good fortune is for other girls. Not me. I'm the girl who finds an amazingly handsome guy, who happens to be a total prince, the day before he becomes her monster stepbrother.

Masking all the mean voices in my head, comparing myself to the woman with pale blonde hair and slim hips, I snuggle up on Rusty and pout. I will have to thank him later for not letting me go or telling me I'm stupid. With unshed tears in my closed eyes, I sink into a blur of temptation and fatigue. I don't know how much time passes before I whisper, "I wish you weren't my brother."

A kiss is pressed into my forehead as I doze off in strong arms that cling onto me like I might actually be of some importance to him. My eyelashes flutter open. The world passes me by in a mass of color. My knees are pressed together and my feet aren't responsible for this motion. It has to be the sturdy arms I'm huddled in, transporting me away from my hellish night.

That's okay. I've already decided these arms can take me anywhere—anywhere but here. I press my lips into warm, rough skin, kissing the neck of my knight in shining armor, inhaling all of him. My tongue decides to have a lick to see if he tastes as good as he smells. Then he growls.

My eyes blast open. "You."

Dustin snares my half-lidded gaze. "Don't look so

disappointed."

He doesn't like the idea of me kissing another man? Well, that's his problem. He should have thought about that before flaunting his sexual prowess in my face. Frantically, I slap at his arm to put me down, but he refuses. He continues to carry me like a groom would carry his bride over the threshold, but the room he enters isn't mine.

"Put. Me. Down!" I demand, like a mad woman.

He drops me on the floor, intentionally.

Asshole.

I wait for him to explain himself, to tell me why the hell I find myself in this god-forsaken room with him, but I would wait an eternity. I don't turn my head, but I hear the door lock behind me. Suddenly, a feeling of terror rips through my middle, but Dustin leaves through the smaller door that leads to what?—the bathroom? I have a quick look around, only my eyes moving across the room, with my ass sat firmly on the floor.

Where the hell am I?

We're alone, the only major pieces of furniture in the room being a large, dark wood armoire and a very inviting bed. This is bad news.

A rush of water catches my attention. My eyes fly to the bathroom door. He's running a bath? I hear his shoes clicking quickly across the tile floors. He peeks back into the room I'm sitting in. I freeze, eyes wide.

"You're welcome to join me, but I can't promise I won't take full advantage of having you naked again."

I sit there stunned for the duration of his bath, but don't dare appease him while he washes the blonde bimbo off himself. Still feeling very tired, and a little sick to my stomach, I crawl over to the large, comfy bed, lose my dress and dive under the blankets in my dainty slip. Dustin joins me a while later, smelling of an intriguing blend of soap and sexy.

Tears pool in my eyes, seeking a weak spot to fall, when I feel his warm arms twisting around me. Having his body wrap me tightly against him brings back memories of things that should have never happened, and my stomach retches, knowing that I can't ever allow myself to have that kind of pleasure again.

I remember Dustin holding me through the night, and I won't forget the comfort I felt, sinking against his body, holding his hand.

"I never meant to hurt you. Please forgive me," he whispers.

And I do. But, when I wake up in the morning, he's gone from the bed, and I fear so is any chance of us publicly being together.

11

Brotherly Love

The sun forces me awake in the morning. My hand pats over the soft, warm space next to me, but it's empty. I drop my head back into the fluffy pillow, sinking into the bed, relieved for once to find myself alone. I sigh, but it sounds like a dying cat. Remind me again why I drank so much wine last night.

I turn onto my side and shoot a pained glance at the oversized patio doors, finding the window naked to the outside world. The sound of rushing water in a sink instantly brings me back to the here and now. Oh, God. He's still here!

This could be my only chance to escape the room with my dignity intact. I shuffle out of the bed and hobble toward the only chance at an early morning exit. I stop and freeze at the window, staring out at the beautiful land. There's only one problem here. I'm on the second floor and there's no way I could climb down this private patio without killing myself. *There's a thought.*

Feeling a little dizzy, I walk back to the bed and sit on the corner of it. The time on the alarm clock blazes, due to blurry vision. My disposable contacts are like crusties in the corners of my eyes. I dig them out, wondering why in the hell the blinds are pulled so wide at this hour in the first place. I stand back up to toss them into the garbage pail, finding a glass of water on the nightstand. It's sitting on a coaster. I lift the glass to read it.

Carver Mountain Golf and Country Club.

Smirking, I gulp the water down and tiptoe across the floor to retrieve my dress and slip through the main door, wearing only my slip, before Dustin even notices that I've awakened. It takes a moment for me to place myself in the building, but once I do, I have no problem finding my room.

Throwing water at my face is a quick wake-up call and swiping the mascara out from under my eyes will do me a lot of good. In fact, I'm starting to feel a little better already as I reapply a small amount of makeup. I smile at the way the shiny gloss on my lips looks and then twirl away to find something presentable to wear, quickly running a brush through my knotted hair as I head back to my suitcase.

Without bothering to attempt another pair of contacts, after dressing quickly, I push my eyeglasses onto my nose and rush downstairs, hoping to beat Dustin to the breakfast table.

I've had better luck.

I have to ask at the front desk where the hell I am, for starters. That's bad enough. Worse yet is that I do this while battling with a migraine from hell. The older woman there is actually quite nice, which doesn't make the situation any better.

"Oh, yes. You must be with the Millers."

"No, I'm just with me," I explain to the smiling employee, realizing my mother is now a Miller too. "Actually, yes. Sorry. I am with the Millers."

I hate even saying his last name because it's the same as my mother's, and makes me feel a little dirty. The kind woman doesn't seem to notice.

"Take your first left and it's the second door on your right." She points in the direction I'm to head. "Go ahead and let yourself right in. They're waiting for you." She smiles, and it eases, just slightly, the tension that quickly refills my hollow tummy. With a nod, I follow the woman's pointed finger, while anxiety balls in the pit of my stomach.

"Thank you," I turn back to say, before taking the first left, while seriously considering making a quick right and getting the hell out of here. My stomach's not doing too well and I'm not that hungry anyway, but the place isn't incredibly huge, and before I have a chance to duck away, I find the room I'm looking for.

The Presidential Suite.

Go figure. I huff when I pull open the door, but it's the only way I can find enough air to get through this next moment. Sure enough, my mom, Jason, and his sons are congregating in the breakfast room. I don't know why this surprises me, but everyone gawks as I approach the long breakfast table. My mom watches me the hardest, the others acting like my lateness hasn't disappointed them, only curiosity making them look up.

"Can you ask your staff to bring down the food now?" my mom asks Jason, who's already lifting the receiver to make the call.

"How'd you sleep, honey?" she then asks me.

Sleep? "Good."

She smiles, recognizing the look I give when I share a half-hearted answer. I just know she's going to poke at me now, even in front of Jason's family. I try really hard to ignore the smirk on Rusty's face and the way Dustin acts as if he hasn't seen me in hours.

My mom wastes no time at all getting into the dirty details. "Did you have a good time last night?"

My eyes flash up to meet Dustin's, but he ignores that, turning to Rusty instead. "What are you looking at?" Then his eyes slide casually toward me, lighting a fire in my chest.

I fear that she knows something that she shouldn't, and my star-crossed glance across the table hasn't helped the situation. "Oh, uh," I stutter, tearing my eyes away from that careless display. "Yeah. It was alright." It's a forced answer that I have a hard time expressing, with Dustin and those full pouting lips sitting right across from me. I remember what it was like to have that sensuous mouth on my neck, my cheek, pulling my lip between his, with his tongue caressing mine and his—

"Dustin?" Jason starts, interrupting memories that should've only happened in my wildest of dreams. "How about you?"

Dustin doesn't answer, but his eyes hook back onto mine. Rusty, knowing all too much, snickers and traps my suddenly desperate plea with a smart-mouthed grin.

He mocks me. "I'm betting Dusty thought it was just as *alright* as you did, hey, sis?"

So, this is what it's like to have a younger brother.

Dustin drops his fork on the table and it clatters to the floor. It's a well-timed distraction, and thank God it works. He stands from the table in search of another utensil, and it feels like I can finally breathe.

"Oh, I can get that for you, honey," my mother insists, rummaging around but not finding what she's looking for.

I stand there casually, gripping onto the back of the chair for dear life, wondering how much longer I can keep up this faulty façade. I notice the second the country club staff slips into the room and in no time at all they're lining the table with food. I don't let go of the chair, only hold it tighter, hoping the others don't realize I'm not taking a seat because I have no intention of eating this morning. Not at this table. Not with these goons.

"It must be here somewhere," my mother insists, pulling open another drawer, growing frantic.

Jason gets to his feet and grabs onto her shaky hand, kissing it, while pushing the drawer closed for her. She looks up into his eyes, hooks her arms around his neck, and gets lost there, instantly forgetting about what she was doing.

"It's okay," Dustin says, with a voice that sounds dry. "I'll get it."

He rounds the long table, drawing my eyeballs back to him. My hands break free from the chair, as he starts walking my way. Boy, does he have balls. What does he think he's going to say to me?

With Dustin looming over me, and the staff weaving around us, the room feels very full. Everyone in the room but Rusty is standing. I keep my chin up defiantly, but my body reacts differently, not allowing me to have any say in how I feel about being this close to him again.

I wonder why Dustin would be so bold with our parents in the room, then, when he quirks an eyebrow upwards, it hits me. The silverware must be in the drawer directly behind me. How stupid am I? I step aside instantly, but he doesn't pull open the drawer. Instead, he reaches behind me, capturing me between his arms. A breath hitches in my throat, as the staff tear out of the room even faster than they had arrived.

My mom returns to her seat, and after a silent prayer, digs in without glancing at us. Once she swallows her first mouthful, she lets everyone know that she sees all. "Move aside or grab your brother a fork, would ya?"

I rush to pull open the drawer behind me, and all the silverware rattles. "Please don't call him that." I dare to look up into his dark swirling eyes. "He's not my brother."

My voice is way harsher than expected and my mother quickly notices that there's a problem between us. Dustin smirks, as if he's amused by all of this, but my mom doesn't get it. She instantly becomes defensive in his favor.

"He *is* your stepbrother, so you might as well get used to that."

I grip the fork with way too much force. When I realize Dustin's reaching for it, I suck in a breath. He can't touch me, not in front of our family. And he doesn't, reaching past me to grab a napkin, the scent of his warm, masculine body making me close my eyes. The brush of his arm against mine is enough to send me into a whirlwind of pleasant memories. I quickly pull away and notice the way everyone watches me now.

"What?" I snap.

My mother stares at me, expectantly. It's not until her gaze falls to my hand that I realize the problem.

Dustin loops an arm around my body and takes the fork from my clenched fingers. "Thanks, sis." He drops a peck on my cheek, discreetly touching me in ways brothers and sisters should not touch.

I scowl at his back as he saunters away, back to his side

of the table.

My mom doesn't look very happy with me. "Lighten up, Izzabelle. Have something to eat," she insists, not understanding the situation at all. "We have pancakes."

"I'm not that hungry."

She points at the basket of fresh fruit. "No excuses. Sit down." She pours me a glass of freshly squeezed orange juice and places it in front of the empty chair across from Dustin. "You're eating something." And I know now, she's not going to take no for an answer.

I scowl at Dustin as I take my seat and scour the fruit for something edible, hating how perfect everything is at this god-forsaken country club. There's not a single bruise or mark on the fruit. Ignoring the fresh cut strawberries and pineapple, I reach for the dark red apple. I spin it around in my fingers, finding it bruised on the bottom. Hah! They aren't so perfect after all. Smiling devilishly, I gently return it in exchange for a long, yellow banana.

"Damn, woman. Could you not have picked another piece of fruit?" Rusty teases.

Dustin laughs with him, at my expense.

"Will you both shut up, please? I have a headache." I pry open the banana with three swift tugs and chomp off the top of it, watching Dustin's mock horror as I devour it.

"It couldn't have been all that wine you were drinking last night, Izzabelle," my mother murmurs, schooling me. "All good things should come in moderation."

Dustin's foot finds mine under the table, just as my insides tighten. My breath catches, making me choke on my banana. I pound on my chest with a closed fist, but it's even harder to stop coughing when I see Dustin lick his lips, like he's ready for me to devour him in that way. Pulling my foot free from his, I get to my feet, guzzle down some water, and then cough some more. After a sip of orange juice that manages to settle my throat, it seems that I might actually be able to breathe again. Everyone continues to watch me, like I'm a spectacle, until I return to my seat.

In silence, I finish the rest of my banana and toss the peel onto my plate. I am so done here. I lean back in my chair and stretch for the sky, hoping the rest of them will wrap things up quickly so I can end this nightmare.

"How do you like the maple syrup?" my mother asks Dustin, making conversation. "Izzabelle tapped that very same syrup right from a maple tree up in Canada last year."

"That explains why it's so good," Dustin answers, folding the wet pancake into four and tilting his head to bury the entire thing in his mouth.

When he knows he still has my undivided attention, my eyes focused on his lips, he slides his fingers into his mouth and sucks them both clean, his gaze burning with desire as he answers. "My second favorite flavor." His eyes drive into mine as his tongue slips between his lips to lick up the syrup.

Just thinking about the things I let him do to me—holes I've let him touch and fill—has me twitching in discomfort, my entire body growing incredibly warm. I chew on my lips and cross my legs, cutting off the circulation. I uncross my legs as the chair scrapes out from beneath me.

"I'm so sorry," I tell Jason. "Please excuse me," I beg my mom from the door, as I rush through it, tearing my eyes away from my new family.

I can't take it anymore. The embarrassment. The desire. The deception.

My mother chases me out of the room, leaving Dustin, Jason and Rusty sitting at the table, stunned to silence.

12

Dusty Knows Best

Dustin

I knew licking my fingers like that was going to rile her up, but I didn't think Izzy would actually leave the room. I didn't want to upset her. I just need her to know that I haven't forgotten about us and I liked what we shared—I mean, really liked.

After another moment of silence passes, my dad commands the table.

"One of you are going to tell me what's going on here." He glances at Rusty, but his eyes land on me. He looks me right in the eye, knowing I won't lie to him.

I fucked your new daughter. It was the best pussy I've ever had.

To hell with that. I'm not going to be the one to break the news. I turn away, pleading the fifth.

Dad turns back to Rusty. "Am I missing something here?"

"Don't ask me," he jabs. "I'm not the one sleeping with my sister."

My dad drops his fork on his plate making a dramatic clang linger in the air between us. I keep my head down, hoping he'll get over it quickly, but no. He dives right in face first. He slams his fists on the wooden table, raising his voice.

"Out of all the women in this city, you had to pick my wife's daughter?"

I fear for my life, but feign boredom. "Will you just drop

it, please?"

But he doesn't.

He slams his fists on the table again and all the food bounces in its dishes. "She's one girl, Dusty. Not for you, at all. She's quiet, sweet, intelligent," he explains, before groaning with disappointment. "You know, I thought she was pretty smart. That is, until today."

What am I supposed to say to that? I did it, and I plan to do it again.

My dad looks completely confounded by this new development. "Dusty, what the hell, son? She's a librarian, you know. She doesn't go out. More nights than not she's got her nose in a book. Can you see yourself living with that for the rest of your life? Because this isn't even worth the argument if you can't." He buries his face in his hands, trying to sort things out in his own mind. "What am I supposed to tell Sarah?"

Avoiding every word he says, I start with the truth, no matter how much it hurts everyone. "I think she could be it for me, Dad."

Rusty laughs at me.

"Did I say something funny?" Anger resonates in my chest, and it takes all that I have not to pummel Rusty's face with my fists.

My dad's hand falls from his forehead to pinch the bridge of his nose, with downturned eyes and his head shaking. "Are you talking about love, Dustin? Let's be real here for a minute. I know that can't be it. You've known her for all of twenty-four hours."

"Actually—"

"Wait," my dad says, intercepting my admittance that the wedding isn't the first night we met. "Do I even want to know?"

I shake my head, while Rusty remains conveniently silent, for once.

My dad sighs harshly. "Do you even know what the word *love* means, son?" His fingers still cover his eyes, like he's hiding from someone, then he swipes that hand through his hair out of frustration. "Love is more than the sweet piece of ass you pick up at a bar. It's more than the little bucket of fun you drag home from a wedding. Love, son, is something else entirely. It's determination and compromise and forgiveness. It's time and effort and money—so much money. Do you think you're really ready for that, son? Because if you think she's it, you'd better think again. What you want and what she wants are two very different things, that I am sure of."

I flash a look of concern at my brother, who's smirking it up. "What?" I snap, my anger rushing right back to a boiling point.

Rusty shrugs his heavyset shoulders, without wiping that smug look off his face. "I never said anything."

My dad pushes out his chair and flattens his palms on the table top, regaining my attention, looking me directly in the eyes. "You're not doing this to the poor girl, and you're most definitely not doing this to Sarah. You'll apologize for the bad judgment and we'll all move on from this."

I turn back to Rusty to avoid the awkward stare of my determined father, but it's no shocker when he decides to add his two cents to the conversation.

"Ask yourself this," Rusty starts. "Are you ready for all that shit dad says . . . with your sister?"

I stand up abruptly with a finger pointed in his face, hovering over the table menacingly. "Fuck you, Rusty!"

With his two middle fingers pointed to the ceiling, he taunts me. "Fuck you too, brother."

My growl explodes through the room as I stomp away, releasing all of my pent up frustration, nearly taking off the door when it swings open and bangs off the wall.

I head straight for the black muscle car parked in my spot, like I'm on a crash course that I can't wait to complete. Turning the engine over, I ignore the loud music and rev the gas, peeling out of the parking lot, leaving nothing but a smoking trail of burnt rubber behind.

13

Back to the Breaking Point

Izzabelle

Leaving the breakfast room was the only answer. I can't bear to be there for the moment my mother finds out what's really going on here. It's humiliating enough. I don't need her chastising me in front of the others. The loose legs of my pants swipe against each other as I try to put as much distance between me and that beautiful, alluring man. By the time I reach the garden, my breaths catch up to me.

I turn away from the table of guests and let out the cringe that I'd managed to save until just now. I thought I was alone. I was wrong.

"Is everything okay out here?" my mom asks, stepping onto the patio and walking up behind me.

I take a deep breath, paste on a smile and hope for the best, turning toward my mother. "Everything's fine."

She sighs, with a look of exasperation on her face, knowing that's just not true.

It's too much. I can't say it. I can't admit this out loud.

A tightness in my chest stops me from saying anything more. A pained expression passes over my face. My mother knows that look.

"Oh, honey. Come here." She opens her arms to me and I step into them.

"Please don't be mad at me," I say softly.

"I'm not," she whispers, soothing me with a steady hand rubbing my back and her chin on my head.

I don't think she quite understands what she's saying. "That's because you don't know yet."

"Know what?"

"Oh," I groan, drawing out this experience with the unpleasant sound coming from my mouth. "I really don't want to tell you this." My dinner from last night rolls around in my belly as I pull away from my mom and step aside.

I can't do this face to face.

"Does this have to do with Dustin?" she asks, a perfect lead into this terrifying conversation.

I spin around, curiosity getting the best of me. "What makes you think that?"

"Honey, I found his T-shirt in your dirty clothes basket yesterday morning."

"Oh." I swallow the warm lump from the back of my throat, but it bobs back up. "I found it on my floor," I admit, nearly adding, "I didn't know it was his," but biting my tongue instead.

I turn away again, and look out over the golf course. I can't lie to my mother's face and she knows it. I feel horrible enough as it is.

"So, you're not sleeping with him, then?"

"Mother!" I snap, more out of horror than disappointment. Has she really figured this out on her own?

The patrons relaxing at a nearby table stare at me, so I press my eyes shut to hide from them. Closing my eyes is always a bad idea these days. I can get lost in my memories forever. Dangerous memories. Powerful memories that screw with my morals and set me back a lifetime. The darkness in my eyelids takes me back to a special time, just last night, when Dustin crawled over me and kissed me from behind after his bath. How I grinned widely and turned my head to the side to accommodate him as he took his time breaking ground and making me his again, starting with soft kisses and strong hands and ending with me calling out his name and clawing marks into the headboard.

When he takes me deep, he seals his lips to mine and swallows my gasping moan with one of his own. I arch my back further and he slides that much deeper—his kiss mimicking the depth of every stroke. He brushes the hair from my eyes and shows me how gentle and passionate he can be while completely consuming me, body and soul. Holding my sleepy stare, he promises, "The blonde—I didn't touch her. She was a distraction for our parents. Nothing more. Never more, Izzabelle."

My heart has never felt so full.

I huff out a breath as I return to reality, my eyes connecting with my mom's. She's now staring at me critically.

Am I in trouble?

"Oh my God," she squeals, catching the attention of the couples on the patio again, and then whispers, "Honey, are you in love?"

I wince from her uncanny ability to read my mind, as I finally admit it, with a soft pout. "With my stepbrother."

14

Permanent Disaster

Five whole days. . . The amount of time my mother has been remarried already. The number of days it has been since I've seen Dustin. The total time I've spent cooped up in my house moaning over the fact that I've fallen for my stepbrother.

The days have been long thanks to the obsessive way I've been watching my phone, my mother's phone, and the door for that matter. I still haven't heard from *him*. Not a single word. I overheard his name once, the other day, when my mom was talking to Jason about the country club, but the second I stepped into the room, they both zipped their lips like it was a secret I'm not privy to.

It's like *we* never happened. It's like our relationship never existed. It's like, I'm going to lose my mind if I don't stop thinking about him every single waking moment of my life. I hear a song, I think of Dustin. I wash my hands, I think of Dustin. I see a pencil, I think of Dustin. Everything—and I mean everything—reminds me of Dustin.

Searching out my mother's favorite yoga show on YouTube blows some time, but once I get into it, my flexibility only depresses me further. The soreness of my body is already fading and so are my memories, like they were merely a concoction of an overactive imagination, although I know from the bottom of my heart that there's no way *all that* was unreal.

Dustin is real.

I turn off the yoga program, deciding exercise was a

dumb idea anyway, and head for my mother's bookshelf instead. Reading has always been the quickest and easiest way for me to forget about things and, although my mother and I do not have the exact same taste in reading material, I can see now that some of my less than gentle suggestions have been rubbing off on her. Hiding between two Danielle Steels I find a gem. I pick up the latest Sylvia Day novel and smile.

"Izzy, everything okay?" my mom calls out from her bedroom.

I head down the hall and peek in the room, lifting my oversized T-shirt over my nose to wipe the light sweat from my upper lip and flashing her the book. Why I thought I'd want this week off from work is a mystery to me now. That was before I knew they were leaving so soon for their honeymoon.

"I'm good," I tell her, as she glances up at me. I drop the book to my side. "Just missing you already."

The tense smile on her face tells me that she doesn't buy it, but then that look softens in an attempt to comfort me. "I'll miss you too, honey, but it'll only be ten days. I'll be back before you even notice I'm gone."

"I'm so jealous. I would love to have traveled Europe with you." I toss the book onto her dresser and move toward her bed.

"Well, when you get married someday, maybe that someone special will want to share this experience with you, and I'll feel a lot better knowing I didn't take that opportunity away from him."

A stab of disappointment has me hunching forward. I pass it off as a side stitch, digging my fingers into my side, with my thumb wrapped around my hip. My mother doesn't comment and I internally thank her for it, regaining my upright stance, while she continues to double check her carry-on bag.

Avoiding the topic of marriage, I say, "Mom, you've checked your bag five times now. You haven't forgotten anything."

She noses around the inside of her bag. "I just want to be sure."

"Jason's been waiting in the car for five minutes already. I think you should give him a break and get on the road. I know how he likes to be early, and you don't want to be responsible for his anxiety attack," I tease.

Zipping up her bag, my mother walks toward me. "Sometimes I forget who the mom is here." She hooks her arm around my neck and kisses my forehead. "There's plenty of cat food in the cupboard. I'd like it if you could scoop the litter every day. I've left extra bags on the counter. I doubt Muffin will come out much. She's not one to cuddle."

"I know the drill, Mom. Muffin will be fine. I promise to check in on her lots."

She hands me the keys and smiles, but I'm not sure what she's thinking, until she says it. "No parties while I'm gone."

I purse my lips as I drop the keys next to the book. Have I ever been known to throw a party? *No.* Do I have many close friends? Not enough that would have me call any event I hold a "party". The only time I go out is for my adult book club and that is one night a month. Even then I always remain quiet and introspective. My mother knows this.

"I'll try to rein in my friends' disappointment," I joke, but my mother sloughs off my sarcasm.

"I mean it, Izzy. No funny business in my house, please. If you want to do that sort of thing, take it to your place."

I slap my hand over my eyes. "Oh, Mom." I can see it coming. When I peek through my fingers, I suddenly wish I had stayed hidden. She's holding out a condom to me. *Not again!* We've been over this so many times before.

"Take it, Izzy. I know you're not on birth control, so I need to know that you're going to be safe about it."

I snatch the small silver packet out of her hand, knowing she won't accept anything less. Not like I'm going to need it. Dustin hasn't called, which I can only assume means that I am forgettable. I find myself squinting to read the fine print on the packet in my hand. Is it an extra-large? I doubt she thought about that before offering me protection.

My face turns ten shades of red, when I realize my mom's waiting for me to explain what I'm looking for. I don't dare say.

"I promise not to do anything within these four walls ever again."

"Oh, Izzabelle. Too much information." She's frowning now.

"We didn't have sex, but—" I start to explain.

My mom stops me with a big palm sticking out like a stop sign. "It's fine. You're an adult, and I don't need to know the details."

I swat her hand away, gently. "You have nothing to worry about. It was obviously a mistake and it will never, ever happen again." I toss her the condom. "I won't be needing this."

She tosses it back to me, making me catch it. "Don't give up so quickly. Ten days is a long time, and if Dustin is anything like his father, he doesn't understand what time means to a woman. He's a hard-working man, Izzabelle. From what I hear, you're not in the clear just yet."

From what she hears? Has Jason been talking about us again? More importantly, has Dustin been asking about me? Last I heard, Jason was taking the news about Dustin and I a little hard. Jason's idea of a happy family involves Dustin keeping his hands to himself. He'd prefer that we never see each other again romantically. The fact that Dustin hasn't reached out to me in five days leads me to believe he has no intention of going against his father's wishes. A frisson of excitement gives me second thoughts.

"I need a drink of water," I say, ignoring my mother's knowing smile, all the while refusing to make eye contact with her.

I rush toward the kitchen and pull open the cabinet housing the glasses. I go up on my tippy-toes and reach for a glass on the top shelf, with my head in the clouds. Such a dangerous place to hover. But what if Dustin knows that our parents are leaving for their honeymoon today and stops over for a visit?

I return the orange juice to the fridge and take a hurried gulp from my glass, wondering what I would say to him if he were to show up out of the blue. There's a knock at the door. I spew the color orange all across the white tiled kitchen. Reality waits for my eyes to return to their sockets. I grab a long stretch of paper towels and drop to my knees to frantically sop up the mess now dripping from the countertop.

This all happens as my mom hollers, "I'll get it!"

It's okay. You're okay. It's probably a door-to-door salesman. Dustin doesn't even know you're here.

Yeah, keep telling yourself that.

I throw the orange towels into the garbage and avoid the tacky stain on the floor on my way to the stairs. The rest of the mess will have to wait until later, when my heart stops ripping from my chest. I tiptoe up the stairs like I'm a criminal in my mother's home. Then I hear his voice. It stops me in my tracks.

It *is* him.

Eep!

"Hi, Mrs. M, is Izzabelle here?"

Fuck, shit, fuck.

Sneaking a glance at the door, I see the way my mom swats at him, giddy from hearing her new title, as she pulls him through the doorway. "Come on in. I'll get her for you."

Look at the way he fills the door when he steps inside. His smile is so disarming. His voice is so charming, and look at how his biceps bulge from his short shirt sleeves.

I can't believe he's here for me!

Creeping up the last few stairs, I take a giant step toward my old room and flatten myself against the wall, concentrating on long, deep breaths, one after the other. Every beat of my heart drives adrenaline through my limbs, making my skin tingle with exhilaration.

This is really happening right now.

My mom appears in the archway at the base of the stairs. "Dustin's here to see you, honey." She says it softly enough, but my heart jumps in my chest. I nod repeatedly, trying to convince myself that this isn't a dream.

"*I know!*" my mom mouths. "He's cute, too." Her voice is soft when she winks at me, but I'm so mortified by her admission.

"Mom," I moan, as I trudge down the stairs racing through the possible scenarios here.

I'm not even controlling my own limbs anymore, because on one hand I want to see him, but on the other hand I want to run far, far away. I'm surprised Jason even let him come up to the house.

"Oh, stop," my mom teases, whispering to me when I reach her. "He's a good looking young man, and you could do a lot worse."

I didn't think she would be so understanding, especially after hearing Jason's take on the matter. I smirk at her now, accepting her hug, as she tells me she has to go. "Take care, honey."

"Okay, have fun. Don't worry about me or Muffin. I have everything under control." I breathe in deeply, preparing myself for what's about to happen. Who am I kidding? I will never be ready for this.

"I hate being such a bother, but the cat needs food and the nosy neighbors need monitored." She kisses my cheek.

"Yeah, especially now that the whole town knows you've married into a filthy rich family." I'm careful not to let the filthy rich man in the living room hear me.

"You saw the papers, too?"

"How could I miss it, Mom? You made the front page."

"We'll save that talk for another day. I have a feeling there will be more of that in our future. But for now, I have a list of emergency numbers here." She hands me a short list. "If you run into any trouble while we're gone, Jason said you can call Dustin or Rusty and they can help you in a bind."

I nod and smile. "And don't worry about Muffin. I promise to pop in often to check on her."

"Okay, I better get going." With a kiss to my forehead, she

disappears to her room to retrieve her carry-on bag. "Lock up for me when you go?" she asks, and then exits the house with a quick goodbye to Dustin.

"Okay. Have a good time," I call out to her.

My mom smiles and waves as she exits the front door. I take a deep breath and psych myself up to see what Dustin wants. *You can do this!*

I peek around the corner first. He's sitting on the sofa, with legs so long that his knees are higher than those thick, muscular thighs of his. I want to slap myself for noticing as he nearly snaps his neck to look at me. Momentum carries me into the living room. I'm hoping my gawking wasn't too obvious.

"Hey. Can we talk?" he asks. "I feel the need to apologize again for the other day."

An apology? That's all he wants? I ignore the way by body responds to him. "What more is there to say?" I barely hear Jason's car as it leaves the driveway, thanks to the blood rushing through my ears.

"Will you have a seat?"

I shake my head. "No, I'm good." There's no way I could sit next to him and keep a clear head. My knees are already knocking and my hands want to wander over his bulging arms, or to his chest to have a feel. I know it's the wrong way of looking at things. No matter how right it feels when we're together, it's just wrong. Explaining our relationship would be a permanent disaster.

He steals my attention with a growl, as he stands to his feet. "You were mine."

My insides tighten deliciously. "Not quite." I try to be quick-witted, but it takes a few seconds for me to regroup from the rumble in his chest.

He steps toward me. "I sure as hell thought so. What changed between then and now?"

It's been five days, and need I remind him of the maple syrup incident? He told me the blonde was a distraction, that much is true, and I might have even believed him, but I've had enough days to convince myself that there's no way this could work out. A relationship with Dustin wouldn't ever be easy. Is easy what I want?

"If it's up to Jason, you'll never get *this* ever again," I say.

With the dirtiest bad boy grin, he tests me. "Wanna bet?"

That threat has my insides twisted in knots. Sensitive parts of my body throb and squeeze. I'm suddenly finding it difficult to breathe as he reaches out to me and runs his fingers down my upper arm. That gentle touch tickles me where it shouldn't.

"Stop with that, will you?" I beg of him, short of breath. I promised my mom there would be none of that in her house.

"Okay, okay," he says, lifting his hands up near his head, framing his wicked grin. "Just walk with me. Then, if we can't come to a mutually agreeable solution, I'll leave. Please?" He's not beyond begging at this point and that pouty lip can have anything it wants.

I'm in trouble.

15

To Be With You

The idea of walking hand-in-hand with Dustin is intriguing. I'm not used to being seen in public with a man, and certainly not a big, beautiful man like him. I'd asked him to excuse me for a minute, and so I ran upstairs to put on something a little more comfortable—and by comfortable, I mean sexy.

Even though I know this walk is probably a mistake—just another opportunity for him to seduce me into sinning—I rummage frantically through my old closet for some clothes to make myself presentable. Why only now am I realizing that I haven't left behind a single article of clothing that a man would find sexy?

Because I didn't think he would come back.

It's true, at work as a librarian, with a full staff of women, I can get away with some pretty mediocre fashions. My teenaged years were no better. I'm afraid the best I can do today is the tight black spandex pants I'd thrown on before I came over this morning. But this sweaty, extra-large T-shirt that makes me look like a blimp really has to go.

Zeroing in on the old dresser flattened up against the wall, I pad toward it and pull open the first drawer. *Nothing.* The second one is filled with my mother's knitting supplies. If memory serves me correctly . . . *Jackpot!*

In the bottom drawer I find a stash of my favorite T-shirts from college. Sitting right on top of the pile are my three favorites. I remember them being a little on the tight side in the chest, which is why I left them behind when I moved out, but they beat the slobby look I'm donning now, so I pull out the T-shirts and decorate my bed with them.

Talk wordy to me.

I like to party and by party I mean read books.

A dirty book is rarely dusty.

Without spending too much time fretting, I decide on the white one and toss the others back to where they came from. Reaching for the door, I swing it open and then proceed to pull on my shirt as I rush down the stairs. When I realize Dustin's waiting for me—watching my hips when I appear at the bottom of the stairs—my breath hitches and I quickly cover my bare stomach.

Dustin acts like he's never seen black spandex before. His eyes linger on the curve of my waist and it feels like he's pouring boiling water down my core. I swallow to wet my throat, but the heat doesn't leave my flesh.

He growls and looks away, and then turns back to me. I push the glasses up on my nose to get a better look at him. He stalks forward, slowly, like a lion ready to pounce, and he doesn't stop until we're close enough to touch. I don't know why but that makes me extremely nervous, making me slant my head downwards. My eyes fall to the floor.

"How about that walk?" he reminds me, my body tightening from the idea of doing anything else with him. He gets right close to my face, forcing me to meet his eyes, as he pushes the glasses up onto my nose, mimicking my own nervous reaction. His eyes drop down and settle on my lips.

I'm not breathing.

His hands find my hips and grip me gently, before sliding up the curve of my waist and resting just under my T-shirt. A blush settles over my entire body. This is where I'm supposed to push him off me and tell him how wrong this is, but my body trembles for more of his touch. He smiles wickedly and his eyes fall lower yet, to my chest, before they return to my face.

"That shirt. I like it," he says, smirking.

Is he teasing me?

I spin away, so I can be free from his scalding hot hands

and hide my arousal and embarrassment. He chuckles at my overreaction, turning away from me and taking a direct route to the door. I twist back around and fall into step behind him.

"What's wrong with my shirt?" Stopping right behind him, with hands propped on my hips, I wait for him to comment.

He twists around, his gaze landing on my chest again, right where the fabric is pulled tight. My nipples harden from the carnal scrutiny and the room seems to warm three degrees. I swallow, still waiting, while he takes his leisurely time ogling my chest.

"A dirty book is never dusty," he reads, then his left eyebrow lifts up.

I fluff him off. "What's your point?"

"You like to read dirty books?"

His voice is low and gravelly. He doesn't even have to try to be sexy, he just is. Although overall I'm feeling agitated, my nipples appear to be extremely aroused by his steady perusal of my chest. I slap my right hand across my breasts and squeeze onto my arm, covering up what he does to me.

"So what if I do?" Liking romances with a tasteful touch of sex in them is not a crime. I lift my chin up, defiantly.

He steps toward me again, a threatening force to be reckoned with. I feel like squealing, but I don't cower.

"You do realize my nickname is Dusty, right?" He pins me with a molten hot gaze. "You wouldn't even need your lady porn if you had me."

Oh shit. Shit. Shit. Shitty.

He leans forward. He's going to kiss me, and . . . I. Can't. Stop him.

The door knob jiggles and the door swings wide without any further warning. My mother's slightly hunched as she retrieves her key from the handle, but her eyes drive right into mine with a delicate *"o"* shape to her mouth. She's frozen in place, unimpressed with what she thinks she's walked in on.

No. No. No!

I swiftly turn away with my arms folded over my chest to hide my aroused nipples. How can I even face her right now? I want to curl up and die.

"Hey, guys. Sorry to interrupt, but Jason forgot his luggage keys in the other room." She makes a mad dash for her bedroom as I scrunch my eyes together, painfully aware of the way she regards me as she passes. It doesn't take her long. She's back at the front door in a matter of seconds. "See? Got the keys." She flashes them to me, as if I might have doubted her. "Okay. I guess that's it, then. Remember what I said, Izzabelle." She delivers the full force of her stare and then reaches for the door. "You two take it easy on each other."

Both Dustin and I notice the way she cringes when she realizes that we could have taken that the wrong way, which I did.

"Just go, Mom!" I plead. "We get it."

She nods, apologetically, then blows me a kiss. "Be good."

I shoot her a slanted smirk, and she raises her hands in surrender. "Okay. I'm going."

Finally!

Dustin's smirking, too, when the door seals shut. I feel his eyes on my face, but I don't dare look his way. "Your mom knows."

Leaving my arms over my chest, I purr back. "And your dad doesn't?"

Everyone who matters knows!

He nods his head. "Hell, maybe I should just put an ad in the local newspaper and get it over with."

My nose scrunches up when I picture how embarrassing that would be for me. I can just imagine the headlines:

Local librarian lands in stepbrother's bed.

There would be an up-close picture of my ugly face taking up the entire front page. I can see it now. I'm sure the future headlines, when it doesn't work out, would be even worse.

Local librarian's lingering obsession with stepbrother.

My heart sinks even further when I picture myself

glancing longingly at him; him with the perfectly plastic blonde on his arm.

The air rushes from his mouth. "Izzy, I'm kidding." He doesn't like the look on my face and he doesn't have to say it to tell me so. The way his eyebrows furrow into an angry unibrow gets his point across. I don't say anything in response. I'm the only one here who stands to get hurt. There's nothing to say.

"We're going. Let's go." He's mad now, taking my hand and dragging me outside against my will.

After he locks up the house, I drag my feet, and his long strides make my feet fall heavily each time they make contact with the ground.

"Would you rather I carry you? Don't think that I won't."

It's his last warning. I take his threat seriously, and quit fighting. The neighbors don't need anything else to talk about. Yeah, I see the way they're gawking at us, even though I act like I don't.

Eventually, Dustin slows down to a snail's pace, without letting go of my hand, and I finally kick up enough dust to keep up with him. I feel the need to apologize.

"Sorry. I don't know what's gotten into me. I promised my mom I wouldn't kiss you in her house."

"You promised what?"

"Nothing." I smirk and glance at my feet.

"Well, thank you for coming," he says, all threat having left his voice.

I nod, smiling softly, no matter how uncomfortable I feel holding hands in public. The idea that this man even wants to be seen holding my hand is an intoxicating one. He steps toward the small park that I rarely see anyone walk through, and I don't complain. I really need to get out of the house more often, although relaxing is the last thing on my mind with this hulking man walking next to me.

Never before realizing how nice it is here, I take in the changing colors of the leaves and the squirrels chasing each other from tree to tree, hopping around pleasantly, hiding acorns. The birds sing a soft melody and the time passes by us as the sun hovers in the warm sky, preparing for its nap.

My hand starts to feel delicate held within Dustin's. His thumb mindlessly brushes over mine and it makes me shiver. The longer we walk, the slower my heart beats, matching the pace of our stroll. I take in a long breath, allowing myself to sink into the moment. Smiling, I bite on my lip and look up at him, gazing into inky, deep eyes. I've never had these feelings before. *Alert. Content. Excited for the future.*

"I'm running out of excuses for everyone, Izzy, and I've decided something today. I'm done with it. If I want to see you again, I will. That is, if you want me to."

He stops walking and I get the full effect of his steady gaze. I blink, repeatedly, like an anxious butterfly, with him reaching out for my other hand. He doesn't know a thing about me, and even though I have it bad for him, I can't imagine saying it out loud . . .

I want to be with you, too.

16

Ruthless

I want to be with you. I need this. We could be so great together.

Even thinking it in my head freaks me out. Dustin watches me go through the motions, trying to bury that unreal feeling that tells me this could actually work between us. He pins me with a hard stare that makes it feel like he's putting his mouth on me. Look at him for God's sake. That big upper body, those dark, brooding eyes . . . and that mouth—

"Everything okay over there?" Standing at his full height, he glances down at me, wearing a deliberate smirk on his face.

Am I that transparent? There's no doubt about it: he knows I want him.

"I was just thinking about *us*," I admit. Not like the park is the place for this conversation, but what better time than now?

A flicker of amusement passes through his eyes before they darken. "I like that."

I steal my hands from his and nudge him with my elbow, because he doesn't get it. "How can you say you want to see me again with Jason being so sure it's a bad idea? You don't even know anything about me."

He reaches for my hand and his gaze softens oh so slightly. "I was hoping to change that today."

With a quick swallow, the lump in my throat lodges in my chest, where it feels like it leaps repeatedly with a thick, speedy thump that I'm afraid he can hear.

"Come. I want to show you something special."

I act unaffected, but my stomach flutters with excitement. He drags me through the grass, and ducks to pull me under the hanging branches of an old weeping tree deep within the park. Once inside the undergrowth, it becomes easier to stand at my full height.

"I bet you didn't know these old trees were hollowed out on the inside."

I shake my head. He's right, I had no idea. But I doubt that blanket just landed there on its own. He had spread it out on the ground and despite having to hunch over to bring me here, Dustin is grinning like a fool. It looks and feels like an enchanted room and his good mood is contagious.

"Dustin, this is beautiful."

He gazes over at me with a knowing look that scares me. "I knew you'd like it."

I answer quietly, letting a soft smile sneak out. "You think you know me."

"No, but I'd like to."

A frisson of awareness skips across my skin. We are so very alone in here. I gasp for a breath when he steps toward me, but then he bends over and parts the weeping branches like he's searching for something.

"Damn it. So much for that." He dusts off his pants as he resumes his hunched position, then dives through the branches, leaving a gaping hole where his body left.

"I can't believe this." He stands outside, looking over the expansive greens of the park, but there's no one there. Who's he talking to?

"What's wrong?" I ask, peeking through the branches and getting a good look at his ass in the process.

"Someone took it." He jolts around and catches my eye. "I can't believe somebody actually took it."

I see him heading toward me and I back away, until we're next to the blanket and he's taking my trembling hand.

"There was a basket," he explains, watching me. "For a picnic."

"For a picnic?" I ask, turning my eyes back to the plaid tassel blanket. It's hard to stay focused with such beautiful eyes studying me. I stare at the red and white blanket. A picnic. Hmm. Here, my dirty mind had me thinking the blanket might be for *other things*.

He cups my cheek gently and tilts my chin upwards, so I'm forced to look at him again. With him hunching forward, our mouths are very close.

"I tried," he says. "I'm really trying here, Izzy."

My words sound soft and curious when I finally answer him. "Why?"

He's surprised, like I should already know the answer to that. "I know you aren't a fan of the family situation, and I've tried to forget about you, like my dad suggested. That didn't work."

I search his eyes. Is this picnic thing his underhanded way of seducing me? Because it's working.

"I was going to try and convince you that I might make good boyfriend material, even if I'm not very experienced in that department, but that didn't work, either. Ah, shit. I'm not very good at this. I don't know what I'm doing here."

Seeing that he has a vulnerable side does not make this any easier for me. "Stop," I say, before thinking about the consequences of doing so. "I can see that you're trying, but there's more to it than persuading me to see you again."

"There is?"

"Can you prove to me that Jason is not your father?"

He laughs, but it's not comical. "No."

"Then the answer is simple really. *We* can't happen again, and seducing me with a walk and a picnic, while a very nice gesture, is not enough. I respect your father and my mother way too much to drop a bomb like this one in their lap. The media would have a heyday with us. You know as well as I do, that Jason will not let this go. He was adamant on keeping us apart. I'm sorry."

I spin around and prepare for the sprint of my life,

knowing it'll be my only chance of survival, but his arms are wrapped around my waist and his nose is in my hair, inhaling me, before I can make my move.

"Nobody needs to know, Izzy. It can be our dark little secret."

My teeth bite into my lip, as he pulls me back against his erection. "This is wrong," I plead, with a strangled cry, but lust pumps through my body from the force of his passion.

"You want me to be your secret? Fine. If that's the way it has to be, then so be it. But you will not make this about anyone else. This is between you and me. I want you. You need me. I'm telling you now, Izzabelle Spade, you will be mine."

17

The Stare Off

Is it okay to pine for a man? What if that man is your stepbrother? What if he is the sexy one, wielding all the power, conquering all your insecurities with a single, menacing look? When Dustin's hand slides down to the juncture between my thighs, my legs give out and he's forced to support the full weight of me. Not backing down for one second, he flips me into his arms, drops to one knee and lays me out on the blanket, crawling over me and teasing with his lips on my mouth.

I find myself pinned rather pleasantly between him and the ground and there's nowhere for me to run. I can't hide from those dark, probing eyes or that hard body that has me aching for him to make us one. Breaths are coming rushed now and I don't know how much more of this I can take before giving in to him.

"Don't tell me you don't feel that," he growls.

I take a ragged breath. Oh, I feel it! That erection has to be the hardest thing I've ever felt pressed against me.

"I want you that bad, Izzy. And I know you want me, too."

A sigh of anticipation rushes from my mouth, giving me away. There's no denying how badly I want this. I do. But it's so bad—very, very, very bad for me to feel this way.

Dustin smiles, like he knows what's going on in my head. "Trust me." He pushes against me, and I shriek from the stimulation, nearly crumbling on the spot. "Look at me when I'm talking to you."

My thoughts stop wandering and I focus on the intensity

in his stare, through half-lidded eyes. My lips part for another strangled breath.

"I'd like nothing more than to fuck your brains out, right here, right now, but I think we need to talk about what happened the other day first, and that can't happen while my dick is wet from being inside you."

My eyelashes flutter up to meet his, shocked by how dirty he's talking to me. Feeling a little feisty myself, I say something that I know will provoke him even more. "Then talk."

With a motion that sends me into a spiral of dizziness, Dustin has me walking ahead of him with his hands on my shoulders, directing me where to go. He doesn't stop moving until we're on the sidewalk and half way back to my mom's house. He stops suddenly with a jolt and spins me around to face him, until we're nose to nose. He's so much taller than me that I have to look up to reach his eyes as it is, but I lift my chin even higher, rebelliously.

A pointed growl rumbles in his chest, suggesting that maybe I'm trying my luck. That sound crawls across my body in a wave of indulgence. I feign boredom, while my body lights itself on fire. One of his hands slides firmly down to my waist, in direct contradiction of his promise to keep our relationship a secret. Once our eyes meet, he refuses to release my gaze.

The longer his eyes drill into mine, my yearning starts to soften and my insecurities start to creep into the forefront of my mind. In public, glowering back with a combination of desire and regret, I grow uncomfortable in my own skin. I try to look away, but his hand slips under my chin and turns it back toward him.

"Look at me," he demands.

I can tell he's about to say something important, so I can't tear my eyes away.

He's so intense. It's terrifying!

"You feel that?" he urges, as an electrical current annihilates my control.

Just the touch of his index finger tracing a line down my

cheek has me twitching with want. I try again to turn my head, knowing exactly what he's talking about.

"Don't look away from me. I feel it too," he admits, his hand weaving into my hair. "That thrill that courses through your body every time I'm near—that sensation is mutual."

I gaze into his eyes, begging for him to stop, but he doesn't.

"I would love to have you as a secret, Izzabelle, but I don't think that's going to work for me." He slowly rains kisses down my neck, stopping only for a breath that warmly tickles the sensitive flesh of my throat. "I don't think you want us to be a secret, either."

I try to break free from him, but I'm not strong enough to leave his embrace.

"Do you remember that night we met?" he starts.

My lips tremble, my knees weak. I go to nod, but instead shake my head, like I'm going to have a mental break down if I think about it too hard. I need to get away, before I fall to pieces, so I pull back from him quickly, leaving a clump of my hair in his fingers.

I can't.

I find myself rushing back to my mom's house, staring down at the sidewalk, anxiety fueling my pace. I walk so fast that it's almost a light jog, until I pass the shiny black car sitting in the driveway and leap up the stairs to my mother's front porch. I try to jam my key into the lock, but it doesn't go in. I peer over my shoulder and notice how quickly Dustin's gaining on me. It's like I'm in a horror flick and I'm not going to escape in time if my fingers don't start working immediately.

"Izzabelle," he begs, stopping at the foot of the stairs, pausing my nightmare.

With an ungodly grunt, I thrust the door open and zip inside the house, standing just inside the door, with it mostly closed. I know he won't cross the threshold uninvited, but it sure looks like he's barely hanging on to his last shred of control. I peer through the crack in the door. He holds my trembling gaze. This is harder than anything

I've ever had to do—ever.

Dustin licks his lips, preparing to make a statement. "You want me."

He says it loud enough for the whole damn neighborhood to hear. I shake my head no, fighting back the emotion that's piling up on my heart. My knees are ready to give out on me when he takes a step closer. My eyes plead with him to stay back, but he doesn't listen.

He never listens.

"I would be good for you." His voice is smooth and soothing, but I can't let him trick me like that. He knows how to use my body against me and it works every damn time.

"I need time," I admit, exploiting how wounded he's left me, before closing the door in his face.

I wasn't trying to be rude, and yet I find myself switching the lock before he tries to hunt me down again and prove me wrong. But he doesn't try the handle, and my heart jumps with pain at the thought that maybe he'll give up on me for real this time. The truth is that *time* will never heal our relationship. He is my stepbrother. Nothing will ever change that.

Being together will never be the right thing to do. It will never be easy. Jason will never accept the fact that Dustin and I need to be together. Even hearing myself saying it in my head sounds stupid. How can two people who only just met *need* anything?

On my tippy toes, I hesitantly peer out the small window in the door, secretly hoping he hasn't moved, but catching him heading back toward his car. He walks with the same confident swagger—that slow and steady gait that makes me gawk at his nice ass. He doesn't turn back and catch me staring, and I'm afraid I don't have the courage to stop him.

It's with a heavy heart and glassy eyes that I watch him speed out of my life, his tires spinning. There I stand, with all the power, but I don't do a damn thing to stop him.

18

Do It Up

Why did I think reading a romance novel would make me feel better? After feeding my mom's cat, I'd locked up, walked home, and pulled out the book I've been dying to read. I flip to the next page, hanging onto every word of it, tears dripping down my cheeks. This was supposed to take my mind off Dustin, but instead it seems that everything is comparable. I slap the book shut. Why must I relate every word to how he acts and how he makes me feel? I sigh deeply, with my eyes pressed shut. I miss him. I actually miss him.

My eyes open, only when my cell phone rings from across the room. My heart leaps into my throat and it's not until the second ring ends that I break free from my frozen response. I scamper across my apartment to grab it off my desk. I don't even bother peering at the screen as I clear my throat and swipe my finger across it maniacally.

"Hey Izzy, it's me, Dustin."

I smirk at that, clearing the emotion from my throat. "I know who it is." Does he really believe I have a long list of men calling me?

"I—uh—I'm sorry. I shouldn't have called. You asked for time. I should give you some. I don't know what I'm doing." The phone goes dead and so I look at it, really hard.

He actually hung up! I can't believe it. But he called. That shocks me even more. The feeling that spreads through me is incredibly uplifting. It makes me feel like a million bucks, and yet somehow disappointment creeps in. As much as I want it to work between us, in the back of my head I fear it never will. I stare at my phone for an entire minute. Watching. Waiting.

It rings. The god damn phone actually rings and the same number pops up on the display. How many times do you get a second chance like this? I don't know, but I'm not going to mess this up again.

"Hello?"

"Hey."

"I'm sorry for hanging up. I just want you to know this is hard for me, too. I know there's a lot on the line."

Yeah, like my heart? Jason's trust. My mother's sanity. The Miller family reputation.

"But I have to do this. I meant to ask you earlier, but we got a little sidetracked. Just hear me out, okay?"

"Okay," I say.

"I have this thing tonight at the country club. My dad booked it months ago without thinking. He was supposed to be there—represent the club. I was planning on going solo."

"Okay," I say again.

"My dad obviously can't make it. I'm next in line and there are two seats reserved at the main table for me. It's my responsibility to make sure the night goes off without a hitch." He pauses and sighs. "I'd rather not do this alone."

I can sense how hard this is for him, but I don't get why. "Your brother?"

"He might make an appearance later, but I'm not taking a man as my guest to our sunset social." He's making a point here and I take it.

As much as my smart mouth wants to ask him whether the blonde will be there, I don't dare. He reads into my silence, quickly.

"I'm asking you, Izzabelle," he states, as if ripping my self-deprecating thoughts right from my mouth.

I swallow. He's asking me—me! I should say no. I should use this as my opportunity to break all contact and tell him I can't ever see him like this again. It's time for me to be the responsible one and put my foot down. "Alright. I guess I don't have anything else planned." I slap myself on the forehead. "What should I wear?"

"The dress code is usually dressy casual. A few people might be wearing jeans, but I'd like it if you didn't. "

"Right." Oh, God. What am I going to wear? How am I going to explain this to my mother?

"I have to be there early to greet everyone. I don't expect you to come for that. I can send a driver for you."

"No, I can drive," I insist.

"Are you sure?"

"Yeah, it's no problem. No problem at all."

I hear his smile through the phone. "That's great. Thank you."

"Like I said, no problem. I think I owe you an explanation."

"Forget about it. I know the feeling. Why do you think it's taken me this long to call?"

"I thought Jason had gotten to you."

"Maybe he had, but I'm making my own decisions now. Tonight will be a fresh start for us."

I cut him off with a gasp, like I finally heard him clearly. "Did you say tonight?"

"Yeah, is that a problem?"

Shit! A little more notice would have been nice. "No. I'm sure I can pull something together." How? I'm not quite sure yet.

"Great. Tonight then."

"Tonight," I say, sinking my teeth into my smiling bottom lip as he gives me the details. The second I end the call, panic sets in. I get to see him again . . . tonight!

Oh. My. God!

I run across the room and throw myself onto my bed, then lift my phone. "Galaxy, call Sadie."

She answers her phone like she's been waiting for me. "Did he call?"

"Yes!" I squeal, not hiding my excitement at all.

"What did he say?"

"You are not going to believe this. He actually came to

see me, but I sent him off. I totally freaked out, Sadie. I can't believe this is happening."

"Okay. You're losing me here."

"I'll tell you all about it later. The point is, he called me back. He asked me out, Sadie! He. Asked. Me!"

"That's great."

"For tonight," I add.

"Tonight?" Even Sadie gets hit over the head with the lack of time to prepare for this.

"Do I really need to repeat myself? I need reinforcements. Get your ass up here."

"What are you going to wear?"

"Oh God. I have no idea. Something dressy casual will do it, apparently, but I think I'm leaning more toward dressy. I was hoping you could bring me some options. Sexy but sensible shoes. And your makeup bag."

"Should I bring the extra-large condoms while I'm at it?" she teases.

"Just shut up and get over here."

"You're lucky I love you. I'll be upstairs in ten. Twenty tops."

"Make it ten. Please make it ten. I'm getting in the shower right now. If you're not here when I get out, I'm coming downstairs to get you . . . in my towel."

"Ooh. I'd pay to see that."

"Sadie!"

"Just kidding. Already know the perfect thing. Be there in a few."

I end the call, toss my phone on the bed right next to my book and unlock my door before skipping to the bathroom. I'm so lucky to live a few floors above my best friend. Moving into this apartment was the smartest move of my life.

Sadie doesn't waste any time lollygagging. She's waiting for me, leisurely spread out on my bed, with her ankles kicked out and crossed when I come back from the bathroom. Laid out at her feet are options. Oh, thank the heavens, I have options.

"Holy shit, woman. How perfect is this?" After slipping on a pair of panties under my towel, I pick up one of the dresses and put it on.

"What do you think?"

She smiles at me. That's a good sign. Sadie isn't one to sugarcoat things. "He'll love it. But do you?"

I check out my butt in the mirror, glancing over my shoulder. Nice. Nice. The navy pencil skirt lands just below my knees, but it fits like a glove, hugging my curves, and the long slit in the back will make it so I can actually walk. I spin around. It's the perfect naughty librarian look. The skirt is sexy and yet reserved, the checkered top sophisticated and smart. It's so me. I like it, but . . . "What about shoes?"

"You could pull it off wearing your brown ones. Or—" Sadie reaches into her bag and flashes the surprise my way. "You could wear these." She's holding a pair of the most fabulous red heels.

"You can't call those casual," I say, as I snatch them from her hands and hop in place to pull the beauties on.

She gets onto her knees, settles her rear on her feet near the edge of the bed, resting her hands on her lap so she can get a closer look. "Yeah, but do you want Dustin to think you look casual or hot?"

The way she exaggerates the word *hot* has me in smiles. The shoes do make me look hot. "The question is, can I walk in them?"

After crossing the room awkwardly, I decide to practice a little more. I'll catch the hang of them, eventually. "Oh, yes. I'm definitely wearing these shoes." I feel sexier already.

"Red lips and a designer bag and you'll be the talk of the town."

I stop smiling and turn to Sadie. "But I don't own a red bag."

She makes a tsk tsk sound with her tongue as she reaches back into her bag of tricks and pulls out a designer bag. "You don't. But I do." She flashes a glance at the clock. "Now do up your face or you're going to be late."

I shuffle to the bathroom and do as she says, paying

special attention to the shape of my eyes. The night will turn dark soon, just like our dirty little secret. Will the others know about our relationship? Will they recognize me as Dustin's new girl or the evil stepsister?

Sadie is the only person outside of our small family who knows about our forbidden relationship and, as much as I thought I wanted it to stay that way, I'm over it. Going out tonight, with him, is me saying that I'm setting the idea of this being taboo aside and I'm actually going to try and give him a real shot. He's got one week to prove that this can actually work, before we have to deal with the wrath of his father.

Yeah, I'm setting it aside, and yeah, Jason is going to be royally pissed, but he's not the only person we will have to contend with. The country club is a prestigious establishment for high rollers, a regular stomping ground for the elite of society. I have no idea how those people will react to seeing me with Dustin. Will they even notice? Fingers crossed they don't. But if they do . . . this could totally blow up in my face.

Please don't blow up in my face.

19

Sunset Social

I'm a ball of nerves for the entire drive and I actually start to second guess my bold choice of shoes when I see the sign: *Carver Mountain Golf and Country Club.*

I pull over onto the side of the long, winding driveway, feeling a little too glossy. I blot my red lips and stuff the tissue into my glovebox, but the mirror shows me that my lips are already stained a perma-red. My insides twist into knots. I'm really doing this.

I put my car back into gear and follow the arrow on the sign that reads "Sunset Social" and pull up past the valet. I think to park where the employees do, then remember how difficult it is to walk in these shoes. I decide to play the part just this once. When I stop my rickety car just past the entrance, it doesn't stall out. A gust of relief passes over me. At least I washed my beast earlier today.

I reach for my bag and strap it over my shoulder as I exit my car. A man swiftly approaches me and grabs the keys right from my hand, exchanging it for a small ticket stub.

"Thank you," I say. This is so crazy. I've never actually used valet before and I can't even imagine him parking that thing in between one of the Escalades and the S8s.

"Have a great evening, ma'am," the older gentleman says, smiling at me.

I nod. "You betcha." Then I turn toward the building and put one foot in front of the other.

The sky is already starting to turn beautiful shades of pink and orange. I know it's going to look amazing from the patio—even more amazing in the company of Dustin. I press my lips together as I show myself to the door. I'm really doing this! Eep!

I try to act like I know where I'm going, but I totally don't. The older woman at the reception desk instantly recognizes me and gives a friendly wave. I wonder if she's happy that I'll be keeping the boss man occupied. I take the gesture at face value and wave awkwardly at her, as I take my time crossing the front lobby, catching a quick breath and scaling the stairs.

I see the doors to the room that lead to the balcony patio and can't help but notice that the people socializing there are dressed more casual than dressy. The men are all wearing khaki slacks and the women aren't in jeans, but they're not particularly dressy either.

I hope I didn't overdo it with the red shoes.

I flip my hair over my shoulder and absentmindedly smooth my hands down the front of my skirt. My nerves aren't getting any better. I swear they're ramping up toward our meeting. I hide my timid smile, when all the guests seem to glance at me in unison.

"Hi," I say, uneasily. This is so not my thing. I don't belong with these classy people. What am I doing here?

I step through the doorway and am instantly offered an apple martini. I smile and accept it. I've come this far. The lights are dim and the room looks extravagant, much like the wedding did. No one talks to me as I make my way toward the patio. I don't recognize anyone either, except for maybe one guy, but he's behind the bar.

There's smooth jazz playing over the hidden speakers in the room and a soft rumble of conversation on the patio. I clench my teeth behind my smile and drum up enough courage to step out there with all those people. Here's the plan. I will go onto the patio, have a look around, and if Dustin doesn't show his face by the time I'm done with this drink, I'm out of here.

I watch my feet as they cross onto the patio, careful not to fall on my face. When I glance up, Dustin stands from his seat, and I only see him. My heart thrums wildly in my chest. He stands firmly in place, like he's unsure whether I'm real. Did he think I wouldn't show? Well, ta da! Here I am!

I must have dressed to his liking, too, because he can't take his eyes off of me. I hate to admit I even noticed, but we match. He devours me, wearing a well-tailored navy suit and tie with punches of red in hard contrast to his simple white shirt. Dressy casual, my ass. He looks like he's walked straight off a men's fashion runway. Holy shit, does he look good!

I lose my nerve, but he makes the first move, leaving the people he was mingling with without a backward glance. He smiles at me, but doesn't say anything, helping me out of my long pea coat as I shrug it off. His mouth moves close to my ear, after he brushes my hair from my shoulder. "You look positively radiant."

His voice whispers over every inch of exposed skin as he tosses my coat over his one arm and offers me the other. After depositing my jacket at the coat check in the main room, he rests his hand on my lower back and introduces me to a few of the guests, who all seem to be showing interest in Dustin's new arm candy. To them, I'm Izzabelle, the university-educated librarian from Carver County. Did he intentionally leave my last name off, knowing how they would react if they knew who my mother was?

Instead of rehashing over all the wedding photos that had magically landed in the local newspaper, I decide that our little secret is safe another day. All of the women Dustin introduces me to are more concerned about their appearance, and sharing stories about their wealth, than making an actual connection with me. They really have no idea who I am.

I smile and keep my mouth shut, accepting the kind compliments from the gentlemen and taking cues from Dustin, like when to laugh and when to walk. After talking to most of the room, we return to the patio and he shows me to my seat, right next to where I'd first found him. He pulls out my chair, and waits to sit until I have. We're seated at a table for eight, the one nearest the balcony. I can't take my eyes off the setting sun, feeling the built-in heaters working their magic, like the burnt oranges and pinks in the sky.

This night is unbelievable. I'm at this extravagant event, with the most attractive man, wearing this gorgeous dress, and no one even knows who I am. For tonight, I can be whoever I want to be. It's almost too good to be true.

Dustin drapes his arm across the back of my chair like I'm his possession. It's not until I glance across the table that I realize it's to stake his claim against the other men seated across from us for the evening. One stares at me a little too long, making me feel uncomfortable. Dustin clears his throat and the man's eyes flash at him before he looks away.

Dustin leans into me and speaks softly into my ear. "I'm glad you came. I was worried that I hadn't given you enough time to get ready, or that maybe you changed your mind about coming tonight."

I smirk, because I had until I laid eyes on him. "No."

He nods and smiles at me, the complete gentleman, giving me all the attention I crave. His thumb sweeps back and forth on my bare shoulder, and I feel that gentle touch everywhere. I try to make small talk with the others at the table, and everything is going smoothly, until Rusty fills one of the two vacant seats next to me.

"Hey, sis," he says, making everyone cock their heads to look at us. He kisses me on the cheek and stares them all down. "What?"

My face quickly goes from a soft pink to a dark shade of red.

"How did you say you met?" a nosy woman prods, showing direct interest in Dustin's answer.

"I actually didn't say." He clears his throat, knowing no good can come of this conversation, but looks to me and smiles like he's not worried in the slightest. He gives me a second for my face to cool, then turns his eyes on the snotty woman. "We actually met at the Ophelia Lounge." His answer is crisp and he doesn't go into detail, but he does grab my hand and kiss it in front of everyone.

Rusty nods his head, fighting off a smirk, like a comedian who can't believe his eyes. "Can I say, Izzy, that you look absolutely amazeballs tonight?"

"Amazeballs?" Is he trying to embarrass me in front of their guests? I can't believe Rusty's acting this way.

Neither can Dustin. He sighs and glances away, like they're not related, just barely maintaining his composure.

"It's okay to accept a compliment, Izzy. You do know what amazeballs means, don't you? It's like amazing— extremely good and impressing. That's you, Izzy. Isn't it, Dustin?"

A darkness rushes over Dustin's eyes, like a dark cloud settling in on an even darker night. There is no question that Dustin wants to bash his brother's face in right now. I drop my hand on his arm and squeeze, tearing some of that attention away from Rusty, so he doesn't do a nose dive into the floor. My grip seems to get the job done and, even though I can feel the warmth radiating from Dustin's neck, he doesn't throw any mean words Rusty's way.

Dustin turns to me and smiles with menacing good looks that make me spin with unsteadiness. "She is pretty amazing."

There's him, and then there's me. In this moment, I forget about the others, gazing wondrously into his eyes. No one revisits the subject of our relationship for the rest of our dinner, and no one comments on the fact that we only have eyes for each other. With Rusty's stupid comments aside, the night is turning out to be everything I had ever hoped it would be and better than I could've ever imagined. I'll never forget the sunset, or the way Dustin massaged my shoulders as he whispered about how he used to sit on this very balcony watching the sunset when he was just a little boy.

I dab my mouth with the heavy napkin from my lap, after finishing the last bite of the most delicious tiramisu, and then drop it onto the table next to my plate. When I tilt my head toward Dustin, I notice he is already watching me. I smile, pressing my lips together with angst and exhilaration.

"Thank you for inviting me. Everything has been wonderful."

He reaches out, letting his hand slide down my arm before entwining his fingers with mine. His smile is all the answer I need, as the master of ceremonies returns to the microphone. Dustin glances back to me with a look of concern on his face. "The night isn't over yet."

I don't like the way he says that. It wasn't in a pleasant way, as I might have hoped. "What's wrong?"

He nods toward the front of the patio, where the overweight M/C is gathering everyone's attention. The older man is wearing a suit. He has a rotund belly but a good seamstress. He flashes a glance at me, and an icy sensation trickles down my back. Ordinarily a man like him would appear smiling and jolly, but his smile is more sinister than angelic. I fear for what he's about to say. Part of my anxiety could be stemming from the worsening grip Dustin has on my hand.

"This night wouldn't have been at all possible if it weren't for the generosity of the Miller family," the man bellows. "Dustin, Rusty, stand up and give everyone a wave."

Dustin doesn't look impressed by the intrusion, and when he stands, he pulls me to my feet with him. His eyes plead with me to support him in this decision, before I even realize what's happening. I smile and lift my hand, as the rest of the guests burst into applause. A few even stand at attention. I've never been on the receiving end of this kind of respect before.

"Wait for it," Dustin whispers in my ear, as we seat ourselves.

The anticipation has me holding my breath. What does he know that I don't?

"Unfortunately, Jason Miller couldn't be with us tonight.

The poor guy got hitched this week." A few people applaud and chuckle, as the devious man looks right at me and Dustin. "I guess he didn't learn his lesson the first time around."

There are more chuckles around the room, but I'm not laughing. If I didn't know any better, I'd say that snide remark was directed at me. Then he confirms my suspicions.

"Jason's new stepdaughter must get her good looks from her mother. Isn't she pretty?" Now he's definitely looking at me, his eyes drilling into mine, like they might penetrate the barrier I've been hiding behind all night. My face flames red, but it's not embarrassment in my gaze. Darts of rage are being thrown from my eyes.

He continues with the premeditated attack. "Go on, Izzabelle. Don't be shy. Stand back up," he insists.

Would it be inappropriate if I shot him the finger? I shake my head and feign a sweet embarrassment, as I smile at Dustin with everyone's eyes on us. The look of rancid helplessness on his face speaks volumes, and tells me all I need to know. This guy isn't done with us yet.

"Aren't they the icing on Jason's cake? I swear the first half of our lives is ruined by our parents, and the second half by our children."

Everyone laughs this time, except for me and Dustin. Apparently Rusty is a bigger person than I am, accepting the insults more lightly. But the guy doesn't stop there.

"I used to have a handle on life . . . and then it broke," he jokes.

I don't know why these people encourage him and his dumb jokes, but they continue to laugh, and so he keeps them coming, while I scowl at them all. People start to notice, too, because they're all thinking about the million dollar question that everyone's dying to ask.

"Hey." Dustin steals my gaze with an apologetic smile. He knows exactly what I'm thinking. "We're okay. I don't care. You don't care. Right?"

I nod, shaken up, because the truth is that I had just

come around earlier this afternoon, and this kind of direct attention terrifies me more than he'll ever know. His hand cups my cheek, his thumb brushing over my skin before taking my mouth against his. He kisses me, chastely, and it's about as comforting as it was meant to be. I sink into his arms, a few stray gawkers eating it right up.

My first dose of relief doesn't come until the ignorant fat man shuts up for the night, but I realize my relief is premature. The nosy asshole from earlier, who is sitting across from me, waits for my undivided attention and starts right in on us.

"So, you two are what?—like kissing cousins, or something?"

"Brother and sister, actually," his girlfriend corrects quickly, blushing when she realizes how rude it sounds.

"Stepbrother," Dustin states. "You got a problem with that?" He has eyes only for Johnson, the lanky man with the big mouth, round bug-like eyes, and puny arms.

The guy smirks, with thin, dry lips, but I can tell he's afraid of Dustin's threat. "Incest is just a little taboo for my tastes. It's not every day you sit at a table with a three-ring circus." He acts like our little secret has just now been blown. "Your father is okay with this?"

"If you're asking whether my father knows we're sleeping together, he does." Dustin says it like he's proud of the fact.

I squeeze my legs together, wishing I could pinch my cool hands between my thighs. Although our family knows, this information going public was not a part of the plan. The Millers have been known to grace the tabloids before. This free-for-all would certainly qualify as juicy gossip. All this commotion makes me a little dizzy and I reach for the table, noticing that Rusty's chair is empty.

Johnson is nodding his head and grabs onto his chin, acting like he's thoughtful, when we all know a nice thought would never come out of that nasty mouth of his. "It's pitiful, if you ask me. You're a disgrace to your family name and an embarrassment to this club." He waves a hand around the room when he raises his voice, like somehow he is the voice of the club and its members.

Before Dustin can respond, Rusty's already hung his jacket on the back of his chair and is grabbing the guy's arm and lifting him to his feet. "That's quite enough, Johnson. I think it's time for you to go."

Johnson rips his arm away from Rusty and spews back at him. "Oh, I don't think so. If anyone's leaving it should be that filthy, incestuous whore. She's not welcome here. She's not even a part of this club."

Everyone in the room turns around to watch the show at my expense.

"We're all adults here," Rusty insists, lifting his hands, seeing the way Johnson's actions are escalating.

A snarl takes its permanent place on Dustin's face, but he holds his tongue, giving his brother the benefit of the doubt here. Rusty pulls on the guy's arm again, and ducks just in time to dodge a swinging fist. Before Johnson can even recover, Rusty's knuckle has connected with the scrawny man's cheek, landing the asshole flat on his ass between two tables. The guests all stare and gasp, but that's about it. Many go back to their own conversations.

If we were at the Ophelia Lounge, an all-out brawl would have ensued by now, but we're not, and nothing more happens, except for Johnson running his fat mouth when security picks the bleeding piece of shit up off the floor.

"You'll burn in hell." He's looking right at Dustin when he says it.

"Yeah, right next to you."

Security shows him to the door, and the crowd applauds when the trash has been removed from the building. Rusty rolls up his sleeves and salutes the crowd of people watching him.

"Never a dull moment at Carver Mountain Golf and Country Club," he says quietly, like he's only talking to a few guys nearby.

The guests nearest to him chuckle and turn back to their respective conversations.

"Please, enjoy the rest of your evening," Rusty announces to the rest of the room. "Drinks are on the house."

He takes his seat as the guests applaud his generosity and rounds of wine and whiskey start pouring from the bar. Now that Johnson has been escorted off the premises, everything that happens after that is rather lackluster in comparison. The music resumes and the glass doors to the patio close as the last of the dinner tables are cleared and removed from the floor, making room for dancing and socializing.

Many of the guests move their party inside, but Dusty and I stay clinging by the patio railing. A chilly wind breezes past us, making me shiver.

Dustin doesn't ask, removing his jacket and resting it over my shoulders. "Are you alright?"

I shift awkwardly from foot to foot. Some of the name calling really bothered me, and that shows on my face more than anything else.

He nods, knowing that nothing is okay right now. "I wanted to kill him," he admits. "Johnson can throw around the word incest all he wants. We both know we're not blood related. But he shouldn't have called you those nasty names."

"All things considered, I'm okay. I think I'm more afraid of what your father will think than anything."

Dustin smirks at that. "Let me worry about my father." He takes my hand and runs his thumb gently over my knuckles. The music has slowed and although I don't recognize the song, the beat ebbs and flows with emotions I'm not ready to face just yet. Dustin pulls my arms over his shoulders and locks them behind his neck, rocking us side to side. It makes me smile really hard, even under these circumstances.

He takes his time pulling me close, and as the song speeds up, he leads me into a dance I didn't realize I could even pull off—especially in these shoes! Others are dancing around us, like the night is still young, smiles and energy flowing like the open bar. My hair dangles down my back when Dustin leans me backwards, swaying my arched body side to side. He lifts me upwards, and I can see that he's smiling now, too.

It's hard to pace our relationship when he shows me romantic gestures like this. He makes me want to throw all caution to the wind. "You can dance." I have no idea what I'm doing, but he's a good teacher, so I follow his lead.

"Lena taught me how to do it right. She always used to say if I ever wanted to woo a woman, then I should learn how to dance." He grins wickedly. "I let her teach me, even though I took a lot of flak from Rusty over the years. He'd always laugh at me about it. Who's laughing now?"

I have no idea who Lena is, and I want to ask him. But when Dustin quirks an eyebrow, quite proud of his skills, wrapping me in his arms and swaying with me back and forth, I lose the need to ask and succumb to the comforting embrace of a man who truly wants me in his arms.

20

In the Garden

As the night winds down, Rusty makes his way over to us and leans toward Dustin. "Did you see that, Dusty? One shot to the face and Johnson will be wearing my fist for weeks. Gah. It felt good. You know how long I've been wanting to do that for?"

"Since second grade?"

Rusty laughs. "At least!"

Dustin stands to shake his brother's hand and slaps him on the back. "I'm glad you did it, because I wasn't going to stop at one."

"Yeah." Rusty laughs. "I kind of got that from the depraved look in your eye."

"Shut up," Dustin says, but he's smirking because he knows he was ready to do very bad things to that guy.

Rusty points an amused glance at me. "I loved it, and all because of our little princess over here."

"My princess," Dustin corrects, squeezing me tightly.

Being possessed by a man so strong and handsome is an intoxicating experience I've not had the luxury of feeling before. While another woman might have felt debased by such a comment, I am proud to be claimed by him. I don't want him to share, and I can't wipe the smile from my face. He's smiling, too.

Rusty tries really hard not to notice what's happening between us before his very eyes, but when Dustin's hand gently caresses my lower back, there's no missing it. I need to gasp for a breath and look up just in time to catch Dustin tilting his head toward me. I cannot believe my eyes. He is going to kiss me—in front of his brother! I know it's nothing he hasn't seen before, but that was . . . before.

This time, when I gasp for a much-needed breath, Dustin's lips meet mine in a soft caress that tears away my last shred of sanity and leaves me panting.

"Hey, guys," Rusty interrupts, noticing the way the guests stare. "I love that dress on you, Izzy. Don't you love that, Dustin?"

Rusty's misguided attempt at distracting his brother doesn't work, and Dustin looks at me, sinking deep into my eyes, pretending just for a minute that it doesn't matter what he does with his brother standing right next to us.

Dustin's eyes flicker down to my mouth. "There's a lot to love." His voice is low and directed toward me, but I know I'm not the only one who heard it.

My breath hitches. I'm now very aware of all the eyes on us. So is Dustin, and yet he threw that four letter word out there for anyone to hear. I don't recall Rusty setting him up for a comment like that. In fact, I'm pretty sure he said the exact opposite of what either of us was expecting.

My burning lungs shatter into pieces, every breath like a sharp slice of air just barely sustaining my liveliness. Dustin's eyes burn with desire, like a raging fire about to wreak havoc on an entire neighborhood.

"Okay, then. I think that's my cue to leave." Rusty quickly moves on to another huddle of guests, and the obnoxious onlookers take their time hovering before getting back to their own conversations.

I swallow, still smiling, but I turn my eyes down to look at my fidgeting hands. I'm not used to this kind of attention. I'm not exactly deprived of love at home, but my family has never shared affection publicly—ever. This is new for me. Is Dustin only doing it to get everyone riled up even more?— give them something to really talk about?

Dustin's not smiling anymore, the look of possession now owning his face. It looks like he's ready to tell everyone to mind their own business, to tell me not to care what anyone else thinks of us. Maybe this really is just for me. The way he's looking at me tells me a lot about how he feels. Above all else, I know he wants to get me alone.

"When I kissed you," he says, "I meant it."

Acting on the impulse I see flickering in his eyes, Dustin pulls me away and leads me out toward the garden. When he opens the door for me, I don't take it as a sign that I am weak, but as a gesture of affection. I can't take my eyes off him, or the steady play of emotions spilling onto his face. His hand clings to his jacket, holding it over my shoulders. Although he's not touching me, the heat of his hands spilling through the fabric scalds my skin, like a phantom burn.

When he stops walking, I start to stumble on that four letter word he used on me—and all the other things he said. Rusty heard it too, I know it. That really just happened. When my eyes meet Dustin's, it's like he's reading my crazy mind. Is he regretting it now?

All the wild expressions crossing his face cease and they're replaced with an honest smile. We're alone now, but still he leans down to speak in my ear. "You heard me."

I force him to look me in the eye, watching the reflection of the stars expand and shrink with every breath. I'm speechless, and he doesn't ask for any words. The soft press of his lips soothes the slight chill of the night, and his warm, sweet tongue seeks entry into my mouth for a kiss that battles for my undivided attention.

He doesn't kiss me for long, just long enough to make my head become one with the clouds and my legs weak enough in the knees that I can't stand still anymore. I turn away to free myself from the stranglehold his desire has over my body, only to see the pool house off in the distance. My pulse instantly quickens and he notices, remembering just as well how intense our passion can be.

"Don't worry. I'm not going to touch you again."

He misreads my response and relief surges through me. I'm not comfortable with the fact that I can see myself falling for him, too. He doesn't need to know that. The sex, though—if he asked for it, I couldn't say no.

"What are you doing then?" What else would bring us out here, I wonder?

"Fresh air?" He's trying to make me laugh, and a feminine giggle sparkles through the night—mine. Now that I believe I'm safe from his wiles, I tease back.

"Are you trying to romance me?"

He smirks. "Is it working?"

I can't lie. "Yes."

"Good." He leans in toward me, and I realize that I was wrong—very, very wrong. He has not given up, only given me a second to catch my breath. He gives me a kiss, and sinks it in deep, making me wonder whether his tongue will be the only thing penetrating me tonight.

His right hand remains cupped gently on my waist, but his other hand finds its way into the loose curls framing my face. His kiss is unguarded, but he's careful not to mold himself to me. He pulls free from my mouth, making a smooching sound echo across the courtyard.

"People are going to talk after tonight," I say, as if he hasn't already figured that one out.

He takes my breath away with another long kiss before answering me. "I've lived my entire life under the interrogation of the guests in this club—mostly lies—and I've survived. Let them talk."

His jacket slides off my shoulders, but he catches it, the heat of our bodies being enough to keep me warm. "I don't care what anyone else thinks, Izzy—only you."

My pulse thuds against my chest like a sledge hammer, when he presses into me, taking my mouth, dominating my entire body with new sensations. His hands cling to my back, holding me against him, his tongue caressing mine.

"I love the way you taste, Izzy. You're so sweet."

I moan when he tugs on my lip with his teeth, a very impressed grin taking up shop on his face.

"I think I've made my point."

I glance over his shoulder and see how every last straggler on the patio watches us, quickly looking away when they see me glancing their way.

Dustin chuckles darkly. "I think we've given them enough to talk about for one night. Maybe I should take you home."

"No. Absolutely not. It's a long drive. I can't ask that of you. I need my car and, if we take it, you'd be stranded in Carver County for the weekend."

He doesn't seem very bothered by that idea. "I can stay at your mom's place. My driver can pick me up in the morning. It's not that big of a deal. Let me drive you."

I still can't believe he has a driver. I sigh, feeling overwhelmed and maybe a little underprivileged. "Or, I can drive myself and save everyone the trouble." Yes, that is what I should do. It's the right thing to do."

Dustin smoothes the back of his hand over my cheek. "Quit looking at it that way. It's no trouble—not to me, not to my driver."

I turn my eyes down to my shoes, and he catches my chin, stealing my eyes from the ground. "You're not trouble, Izzabelle. You're the least trouble I've ever seen. The people stare because you're beautiful and genuinely good. I've snagged the prize right out from under their noses and they're jealous. They're probably wondering what you see in a guy like me."

"A guy like you?" This floors me. He's a lot of things I look for in a man. Dare I say everything? He's tall, dark *and* handsome. Oh, and wealthy—did I say wealthy? Employed. That's another good quality that many men in my shit hole town can't say. Educated. Street smart, even.

He adds a few things to the list. "Jealous. Hot tempered. Pinned to Carver Mountain for the rest of my life. It's my legacy—my responsibility. The country club is mine, just as soon as my dad hands it over."

I shrug my shoulders, surprised that he shares that piece of himself with me, but I'm thinking it sounds pretty nice to have a family legacy. "That doesn't sound so bad. It looks like you've lived a charmed life."

Now he's the one staring at his feet. "Looks can be deceiving."

"Hey, I'm sorry. Did I say something wrong?"

His eyes zoom up to mine, his brooding stare dark and damaging. "If I tell you this, you have to promise you'll never tell another soul."

I think about it for only a second, and admit, sheepishly, "I tell my mother everything."

"Your mother already knows."

That startles me, but I quickly hide that look and nod, because it seems to mean a lot to him. "I promise."

He swallows and shakes his head with disguised bitterness. "When my mother left, it wasn't pretty. She didn't want us kids and she didn't want the house. She wanted money, of course. They always want the money."

I don't like the way he says that, but I don't bother to mention it. "Your dad didn't have a prenup?" Because I know my mom had to sign one before they tied the knot.

"Oh, he did, but he was a fool in love and he gave her more than her fair share of his family's estate—way more."

I'm curious to hear more. Maybe it'll explain why he's harboring such harsh feelings about his mother. "What happened?" I don't actually expect him to answer me, but he doesn't even hesitate.

"After Rusty was born, everything went downhill. By the time he turned two, she couldn't take it anymore. He would cry all the time and so would she. I remember it like it was yesterday. Some called it post-partum depression, but my dad called it gold digger syndrome."

"You were awfully young to remember those types of things."

"I was just little, and maybe it was from my dad's *gentle* discussions with my aunt over the years, but I still remember the day my mom told me I was the reason she left. I was bad, she would say, so bad that she had to leave us. Rusty has always believed it was him who sent her packing. I know it was me. I heard it straight from the horse's mouth."

"That's horrible. I can't believe a mother would ever say something so cruel to her child. What did your dad say to that?"

"I never told my dad about the filth she would spew over a two minute conversation. She was always on her best behavior whenever she talked to him. Once a year or so, she would call, sometimes more often. I expect it was whenever she ran out of money."

"I'm so sorry."

He looks up to me, with glossy, heartbroken eyes. "She just took the money and ran—never looked back. My dad had to sell our house and mortgage a shitty dump downtown just to keep the country club afloat. We practically lived at the country club after that. He was working his life away. He cut staff and hired one of the ladies in housekeeping to watch over us."

"Let me guess, the receptionist?"

"Lena," he tells me. "How'd you know?"

I shrug, proud of myself for figuring it out. "She seemed a little too invested in you—very kind, but observant, and very cautious around me."

"She's the closest thing to a mother I've ever known." His admission tugs on my heartstrings. "Would you like to meet her?"

My heart flip-flops with nerves and exhilaration. He wants me to meet her? Tonight has already been one crazy, fulfilling night. "It's kind of late, don't you think?"

Rusty hollers at us from the patio doors. "Time to call it a night."

Dustin collects me in his open arms and I cuddle against him as we head back through the garden toward the patio. Rusty's smiling as he locks up the doors behind us.

"Why don't you guys get out of here? I'll take care of shutting the place down."

"Are you sure?" Dustin can't seem to believe his ears. This mustn't happen too often.

"I got this, and Izzy has a long ride ahead of herself. You can go ahead." Rusty reaches his arm over my shoulder and squeezes me into his chest. "Sorry you had to go through all that tonight, but if you survived that drama, you've earned your place in the Miller family."

"Thanks . . . I think."

I smirk at Dustin, but he doesn't return the amused look, jealousy smearing the smile from his face. He doesn't like the way his brother holds me. It's innocent enough. I smile up at Rusty, who squeezes me again, before letting me go, knowing Dustin's about to sock him one.

"Goodnight Rusty," I say, as I'm pulled through the lobby by my jealous lover. Rusty just waves, with a silent hand reaching casually into the air.

"Where's Jake?" Dustin asks the woman at the front desk, with a snap to his tone.

It's not Lena standing there anymore, but a different girl and she has my key ring dangling from her finger. "Jake was done at one thirty."

"What time is it?" he asks, a little softer now.

She checks her computer to answer him. "One thirty-six, to be exact."

"Here, give me the keys. She's not driving home. Do we have any rooms available?"

"I'm afraid not," she tells him, as she double checks their system.

I try to settle his mind. "Dustin, it's fine. I don't need a room."

The girl starts tapping on her tablet, then hands it to Dustin. We do have a garden view room free, but it's the last one and I know how you like to keep it open for emergencies."

He glances at me. "I'd say this is an emergency. You've had too much to drink."

I slant a look at him, knowing that the girl is watching me, smirking. "Dustin, why don't I just go home with you, if you think it's such a problem? You can give me a ride back here in the morning and I can drive myself home from here."

He growls in warning. "I don't think you want to do that."

Excitement prickles across my body. "If I'm making my own decisions, then yeah, I do."

He tries to come up with a reason to change my mind, but it's not going to work. I've made up my mind. He hasn't.

Dustin pulls me aside and talks in hushed tones, so the receptionist can't hear our discussion. "It's bad enough the disgraceful looks you had to put up with tonight, I don't need other rumors being spread." He smiles across the lobby and nods at a few guests that had been waiting for their limousine to arrive.

"Are they really rumors if they're all true?" I whisper.

He huffs, growing tired and irritated, squeezing his eyes shut and pinching the bridge of his nose.

"Shall I call your driver?" the receptionist interrupts, hoping it'll help.

Dustin doesn't answer, so I do. "No. That won't be necessary. Thank you." I turn to Dustin, who's now rubbing his eyes with two fingers poking at his sockets. "Can we just go, please? It's late, my feet are tired, and I just want a place to rest my head. Your sofa would do the job just fine, but if you insist on being so bullheaded, I will call a cab and sleep at the Motel 6 up the road."

The receptionist presses her lips together in a smile, waiting to hear what Dustin has to say about that. My keys jump off his finger and land in the palm of his hand.

"Alright, it's settled. I will take the sofa and you can have my bed. The last thing I need is Rusty walking through the house in his underpants, trying to put the moves on you in the night," he mumbles, taking my jacket from the girl's extended arm.

I laugh out loud, as he helps me into my coat. "Have a goodnight," I say to the girl, as he pulls me across the lobby. I throw my purse over my shoulder.

"Goodnight," she cheers. "Take care!"

I take Dustin's arm and he pulls me to the only car in the lot that looks like a heap of metal from the junk yard. He waits for me to get in my passenger door, then closes it firmly behind me. He doesn't comment on the way the driver's door hangs from its hinges or how the ignition sticks when he tries to turn the key.

"Fasten your seatbelt," he orders, as he grabs onto my headrest and looks over his shoulder.

I string the belt over my lap, having no idea how far away he lives, but too tired to ask. I rest my head against the seat and close my eyes, smiling. This should get interesting.

21

You Ain't Getting None

"Izzabelle," Dustin whispers, waking me from a wildly entertaining dream. "We're here."

I mumble my response, turn onto my side and slip back into a deep sleep. When my car door is pulled open, my body falls aside and my eye lashes flutter upwards. He's standing there, dark as night. I'm entranced by the sight.

I'm unable to read his eyes when he takes my feet and gently turns them until they're resting on pavement. I'm a little disoriented, everything is blurry, and my head spins before everything turns back to normal—ish.

"Can you stand up, or do I need to carry you?"

My teeth bite into my bottom lip. I still remember the last time I found myself being carried in his arms. As pleasant as it was, I don't' want him to think of me as the helpless lush. I take his hand and pull myself to my feet.

"I think I'm okay," I tell him softly.

"Good. Let's go."

He takes my purse from my hand and straps it on. I almost die of shock—the most pleasant kind—because this man is wearing my red purse. Am I in heaven?

It's dark, and all I can see is the light on the front porch. We're not at a downtown bachelor pad, like I expected, but a huge family home with a two car garage and a wooden bannister, painted white, framing the entire frontage of the house. Large potted plants donning fall foliage stand on either side of the stairs, like a gateway to a lovely greenhouse. Gardening is clearly someone's passion.

When I look up to smile at him, Dustin has a soft, dreamy look in his eye. He unlocks the door and lets me in first. I wait for him to flick a light switch, but instead he pulls out his phone, shuts down the security system with four digits, and with another swipe of his fingers, the lights flash on, one at a time.

"Whoa." I've never seen anything so techy before.

"It's not a big deal."

I smirk, making fun of my poorness. "It sure beats the chain on my apartment door."

It's apparent he doesn't like me comparing my poor ass to his, but he doesn't voice his opinion on the topic, and I'm hoping it's because he's as tired as I am. I watch him pull off his shoes first, then he drops down to one knee to remove mine.

"You don't have to do that," I say, while enjoying every moment of him looking up at me from the floor.

Dustin carefully removes my shoes and lifts to his feet, collecting me in his arms. He drops a chaste kiss on my lips and lingers by my neck, inhaling me. I close my eyes loving the way he cherishes me. Soon after losing our jackets, we've moved to his bedroom. He lets me go to turn on a lamp next to his bed and then crosses by me to pull a spare blanket from the top shelf in his closet. He places the blanket at the foot of the queen-sized bed and then steals a pillow from the headboard before turning to me.

"You'll be sleeping in here."

"All alone," I add. By the look of it.

"I'll be just outside your door if you need anything. On the sofa."

How awful does that sound? "Can I persuade you to stay?" I smile coyly, with my hands clasped together and my shoulders swaying front to back.

"No," he states, like it's not up for debate.

I tend to disagree. "Then who's going to help me unzip my dress?" I play coy well, turning away from him and glancing at him over my shoulder.

"It's not going to work," he says, although I can already

see that it has.

He moves gracefully toward me, but I stop him.

"Wait. We wouldn't want Rusty walking by and seeing anything," I insist. "You might want to close the door first." I tug the top from my outfit over my head.

That fuels the forbidden fire. He pushes the door closed, but doesn't lock it. That disappoints me. I hold my hair up with both hands above my head. Dustin's fingers slide down my bare back, slowly. The only thing I hear is the zipper and his heartbeat thudding in his chest.

"How's that?" he asks, as I slip my arms through the straps, letting the garment fall forward, folding in half in front of me.

"Could you unhook my bustier?"

He chuckles darkly as his fingers whisper over my spine. His growl is a threat that I find insanely sexy.

After doing as I've asked, he steps away from me. I let my lingerie drop to the floor from my fingers, then turn to face him, squaring my shoulders. My breasts bounce freely, my nipples standing at attention with anticipation.

Dustin's eyes drive into mine. I know he wants to have a look, but he doesn't take his eyes off of mine. I can fix that. Bending forward to unsnap the thigh high stockings from my garter belt, I drop my dress and garter to the floor, leaving me in very small panties as I roll the stockings off my feet one at a time.

I step out of the pile of clothes at the floor on tip toes and spin away to turn down his bed. I lean forward and pull down the duvet first, then the sheets. He watches every wiggle of my ass and don't think I don't know it.

"You're going to sleep naked?" he asks me incredulously.

I know how hard this is for him, and I love it. "No. I'm still wearing panties."

He takes in my smirk then peruses the rest of my naked body. I let him have a slow look, then crawl on top of his bed, resting on my knees, wearing nothing more than the curls draped over my shoulders.

He's scowling at me now, but there's no hatred in his

eyes—only lust. "I'm leaving now, with very dirty thoughts of you in my bed. Goodnight," he says, before disappearing into the darkness near the door.

"Wait," I plead. He spins back to me, but I know I'm not going to win this argument. "Aren't you going to tuck me in?" I try to hide my smirk, but fail.

The smile that graces his lips is promising. He steps toward me, slowly, reaching past me to pull open the blankets. His hand brushes past my breast as he does it. I gasp for a breath then settle under the covers, letting him tuck the blankets around me, hiding the nakedness.

He hovers above my head. "We've had a long night. You should get some sleep."

I nod, disappointed with the lackluster ending of our date, but oddly very content. He leans down and kisses me gently on the lips.

"Goodnight, Izzabelle. Sweet dreams."

I gaze into his eyes, falling into their dreamy depths, accepting his painfully sweet kiss and watching him walk that fine ass right out the door.

22

Broken Down

When I finally get out of bed, I have cereal, even though it's almost noon. Rusty watches the way Dustin and I smirk at each other across the table. I don't even know what I'm smirking about. I'm just happy is all. Dustin had come in his room for a cuddle this morning. It was sweet and I had fallen back into a dream-like state, wrapped in his strong, warm arms. I could've stayed there like that with him forever.

After eating, Dustin retrieves a small overnight bag I had packed in my trunk, and he gives me some space to put myself together. When I appear in the living room, he leaps to his feet and stares at me. Rusty doesn't move a muscle and continues to face the show they were watching, while Dustin tries to keep his eyes in their sockets.

"I'm gonna get going now," I tell them, without making any more eye contact with Dustin.

"Okay, catch you later," Rusty says casually.

Dustin wanders closer to me, with the same gait that had attracted me to him the first night we met. "I'll walk you out."

I nod, accepting his hand and walking toward the door. I pull on the sexy red shoes he had dropped there last night, even though I have flats in my overnight bag. I need Dustin to remember what he's missing out on. I press my lips together, smile at Dustin and turn for the door. He holds it open and follows me outside in sock feet.

I head straight for my car, toss my bag into the backseat

and my purse in the front, whirling around to face Dustin. "Thanks for everything. Last night was . . . great," I say, not mentioning the horrendous rumors that must be flying around today.

Before I can slouch into my seat, he pulls me into his arms and leans down for a kiss. Before our lips touch, he growls. "Don't think you're getting away that easily."

He gives me a goodbye kiss fit for my own personal fairytale, except I'm not a princess and I'm not wearing my glass slippers.

His teeth tug on my bottom lip with a smile. "I'm glad you came."

Even though the skies are grey, he makes me feel like a ray of sunshine bursting from the smattering of dark clouds. I drop into my seat and wiggle the key to get it into the shoddy ignition. Dustin closes my door, pushing it heavily to get it to latch, and it does, but he doesn't head back inside. I wave through the glass, hinting that he can go before the rain hits, but he still doesn't move. He's only wearing socks!

I huff, twisting the key, chanting for it to work, trying with pure determination to get it to start. It doesn't start. I try again, but nothing. I cringe in Dustin's direction, through my window, then put it down to talk to him. The window jerks downwards but stops halfway.

I cringe, again. "It won't start."

"Yeah, I got that much. Pop your hood."

I do and he gets the hood up and has a look underneath. Large droplets of rain start to sprinkle on the pavement, but Dustin doesn't seem to notice. He plays around with who-knows-what under the hood and says, "Try it again."

I stop when the grinding noise doesn't.

He strolls up next to me. "I'm no mechanic, but that doesn't sound very good. Why don't I call you a tow? I can get your car in the shop right away, so we can get you fixed up and on your way. Our guys at the dealership are pretty good. I'm sure I can pull a favor to get you in this afternoon."

"No. No favors are necessary. I'm sure there's a little

shop up the road that can help, and I bet the price will be a lot more affordable."

He raises his eyebrows, noticing the way my chin is held high and my stubborn eyes are set on what we're going to do about this. Still he says it. "It's not a problem, really."

I'm not rolling in a bed of money. I have a decent job, yes, but I can't afford the prices the dealership will want to charge for this little problem. I'd prefer not to dig into my savings to fix my hunk-o'-junk car, if I can help it. "No."

"Okay, have it your way." He raises his hands and leaves it up to me.

My window jerks upwards, hesitating, but it closes, just in time to beat the rain. I Google the nearest mechanic and make the call, while Dustin jogs up his front steps to avoid the downpour of rain suddenly pounding the pavement. I have to holler over the rushing sound of water on my rooftop, but the guy on the other end of the phone doesn't sound very sophisticated.

I wait for him to check his schedule. He can get me in!

"Can you do the tow as well?" I ask, with my best pretty-please voice.

"We'll be there before you know it."

I smile into my phone. "Okay, great. See you soon."

I pull my keys out of the ignition, wait for the rain to slow, and then race up to the front porch where I find Dustin watching the rain, protected by the monstrosity that is the roof on their front porch.

"He said he'll be here soon."

"Soon, as in five minutes or twenty five?" Dustin asks me.

I take a seat next to him, swinging slowly while we wait. And wait. And wait. Two hours later, I'm sitting in his front window, following the trail of the double rainbow in the bluish-grey sky, when I see the tow truck pulling up the road.

"They're here!"

Dustin looks up from his tablet and smiles. "Right on time," he mocks.

I scowl back at him as we head for the door. "Very funny.

What are you doing?"

"I'm coming with you." He doesn't ask for permission.

"You don't have to come. I shouldn't be long." I feel dumb for saying it out loud.

He puts on some shoes and follows me out the door. I'm not complaining, anymore. I'd actually hate to go alone, especially once I see the hygiene of the guy I'll be driving with.

Dustin talks to the filthy mechanic in grease-stained coveralls as he hooks up my car. The guy seems to think he has the part I need and says, "We'll get it fixed up in a jiffy. Why don't you ride with me, and I can get you to fill out your contact information at the shop?"

I nod, my grin disguising my disgust. Dustin talks quietly, so the man can't hear our conversation. "I have to get Rusty to run me over to the club so I can pick up my car. That should give you time to settle up with him. Why don't I pick you up at the garage?"

"You know where it is?" I ask, pulling my purse out of the car.

"Yeah."

"Okay," I say, walking toward the passenger side of the tow truck.

The mechanic smiles at me when I climb into the passenger side of the truck, with slimy teeth and a dirty look in his eye. I don't like it at all, but I put up with it, knowing Dustin isn't far off.

"My boyfriend is going to meet me there," I explain, hanging onto my last breath to keep from smelling the rancid body odor of the man next to me.

As if the smell isn't bad enough, I have to keep my eyes focused on things outside, while trying to ignore the reflection of the dirty man ogling my body. I suddenly wish I wasn't wearing such sexy heels. I'm careful not to get them dirty, praying that he doesn't think me wearing these shoes is meant to provoke his attention. No woman wants that kind of attention from a man like him. I feel dirty just sitting next to him.

It's not that the drive is far, but it feels like the longest ride of my life. I hug my purse against my chest, trying to keep from getting dirty, wishing this horror show would end already.

"You look awfully familiar," he says to me.

I don't respond, my forced smile not looking very convincing.

"Yeah, I knew I'd seen you before."

I cringe internally, wondering when the last time this truck had a bath—like never? Kind of like the driver. Are we there yet?

"You're that girl from the newspaper."

I shake my head as he pulls into the parking lot of his shop. "No, you must have me confused with someone else."

He stares at me, hard, while I try to avoid making eye contact with him. I see another guy working under the hood of a car, and when the truck rolls to a stop, relief overwhelms me. The driver catches the look that passes over my face, but I don't care. I leap out of the truck and slam the door shut.

"Joe," the man shouts. "Look what the cat dragged in."

I scowl at him, not liking his connotations.

"That's my brother, Joe. He'll be the one working on your car."

I nod, deciding not to teach him a lesson in manners. They *are* going out on a limb for me under such short notice, after all. I reluctantly pay the man a deposit and give him my name and a cell phone number that I can be reached at.

"Four hours?" I say with a hard look. I'm just as shocked that I could read his chicken scratch.

"It's not an easy job, darlin'."

When he starts to explain, I hold up a hand. "Thank you. Just call me when it's ready."

I walk off in my red heels, and stop at the curb, considering whether I could make it all the way back to Dustin's house by foot. It'd be a long enough walk in these shoes, but the way the mechanic's brother tips his hat, gawking at me with that same disgusting look in his eye, makes me strongly consider it. I dig through my purse for my phone, but find no notifications for me there.

A shiny black muscle car with a red line running down the length of it rolls up in front of me. The windows are dark, but I know who I'm up against. I flash a look at the black chrome wheels as a dark-tinted window slides down. Dustin is inside, leaning over to see me through the passenger window. He glances at me over his shades. "Looking for me?"

I smirk at him, relieved and excited that it's him. He looks hot, and the car itself is pretty hot too. I get in, remembering why I'm wearing the shoes; they're like my sexy security blanket.

"Thanks for coming to get me. I guess they could be a while yet."

"I kind of figured." His smile is warm and welcoming. "We can head back to my place."

"Is that what your plans were before I ruined your day?"

"Let's get one thing clear: you have not ruined my day." He checks the traffic and slides his car in between two others, with a growl of his engine. Like him, his car is built for getting what it wants when it wants. There's an added power beneath the hood that you don't expect to catch a glimpse of, but once you do, there's no turning back.

I watch the way he handles the stick, like it's a game he loves to play. He makes me want to play, too.

Dustin pulls off his sunglasses and smiles over at me. "What's got you in smiles?"

A rush of heat reaches my cheeks under his amused scrutiny. I don't bother answering. He knows I was checking him out. I'm allowed to do that.

I clear my throat and gently act like I'm not preoccupied by every square inch of him. "You don't have to change your plans on my account. There was a small sitting room at the garage. I could always wait there."

We're stopped at a red light. "I do need to stop in at the club to make sure everything's running smoothly. I was going to pop in when I picked up my car, but I thought better of it. You looked like you needed saving."

"Did I really? So, *I am* upsetting your schedule." I notice how quickly the roads are flying by, one after the other. It's making me dizzy. My head starts spinning, much like my disheartening thoughts. "If you could just turn around and take me back—" A rush of emotions chokes off my voice.

He has other things going on in life that don't include me. He had plans for the day and I've already ruined that. How dumb of me to believe he might actually want to spend more time with me. A dismal feeling starts to set in, that good feeling from our all-morning cuddle starting to fade.

Dustin flashes a look my way before turning the corner. "Hey. Don't be ridiculous. I would never leave you at that dirty place. You'd wreck your shoes."

Although I'm not that shallow, Sadie would probably kill me if I messed up her shoes. Regardless, he's trying to make me smile and it works. With a deep breath, I finish what I wanted to say before the emotions swelled high in my chest.

"I can keep myself occupied in other ways."

He nods, like he's sure I could, but he has other ideas. "I was kind of hoping you'd come with me."

"Oh! Really?" I can't even hide the relief in my high-pitched voice.

"Only if you want to." Once the car is in fifth gear, his hand cups over the back of mine and he squeezes it, his fingers weaving their way in between mine. "I was going to head in to the club to check on things, do a little paperwork, but it's nothing that can't wait until Monday. What does Izzabelle want to do?" he asks. "The choice is yours."

"That is completely fine with me. You have work to do. I will help however I can."

Dustin chuckles darkly. "I'm not expecting you to work, Izzabelle. You can walk in the garden, lounge on the patio, have a drink at the bar, but work? Absolutely not."

"I'll do my best to stay out of your way." At first I feel a bit of my pride slip away, with him thinking I'm a useless little twit, but then I remember how much he cherishes me when we're alone and I know I'm overreacting.

"Are you joking? I like having you around. I thought that was pretty obvious." He checks his blind spot and speeds down the lane toward the Carver Mountain Golf and Country Club. He pulls around the back of the building and drives up to the best parking spot there is, which is clearly designated as the spot for the "Club President". He smirks at me. "One of the perks of being number two."

I smile and nod, helping myself out of the car. I meet him at the back door, where he keys his entry and holds the door open for me. "After you."

"Thank you."

A girl could really get used to this. Does he really mean all those nice things he says? Does he always hold the door open, like the ultimate gentleman? It's hard to believe he's not been put up to this. I'm his stepsister, who usually hides out in my apartment all weekend with a book, or four. I swear I've been out and about more with him in the past couple of days than I have for the entire month on my own. Aside from work and grocery shopping, I don't go out much. I even try to blend those two events into one trip, if I can.

I'm shocked when Dustin reaches for my hand. He's the boss, after all, so I cling onto his hand, feeling a little honored by the gesture. This is his workplace, his employees, his guests, and he's flaunting me around, greeting them all like it's nobody's business, and I'm not some new arm candy that will be gone by next week. Will I be? I hope not.

He looks down at our linked hands and winks at me. "Today is my day off."

The way everyone's staring, it looks like they've figured that one out too. "How do they know this?"

He makes an amused huffing sound, like it's quite obvious. "The jeans. It's not really appropriate club attire."

My eyes grow wide with understanding. They have a dress code here? That would mean that I'm dressed rather inappropriately too, wearing such a short skirt. It's no wonder everyone stares as we pass them. A blush floods down my entire body.

"You're fine," he whispers. "They're not staring because of your clothes."

How does he do that? He finishes my thoughts and answers my unspoken questions. Don't get me wrong, I love it, but it's a slight bit jarring and sends tingles from the tips of my fingers right down to my toes. He squeezes onto my hand and walks a little faster. I feel winded, trying to keep up with him in these shoes.

One turn of the corner brings a new escape for me—an atmosphere I am much more familiar with. There are modern boardrooms lined up on one side of the hallway and smaller offices bordering the other. Most are empty. It is the weekend, after all. The executive wing of his club is quieter than the lobby, a single employee walking toward her cubicle with a purpose, but other than that it is empty— if a hallway filled with luscious plants in extravagant pots and attractively framed paintings adorning the walls can be considered empty.

It's not until we reach the very end of the hall that we're met with a pair of rich brown office doors. They're closed, but I get the idea that the real business happens behind these doors. I glance at Dustin before reading the shiny, engraved name plate.

Dustin Miller
Director of Golf Operations - Management

He smiles and offers for me to walk in ahead of him, and I do, slowly. The back wall of his office has a panoramic view of the golf course, a gorgeous view of the wet, emerald grass and the dark clouds mixing with the icy grey ones. The entire room breathes like it's alive, framed by the wonder and tranquility of nature.

"This is amazing."

"My dad's is just as nice." Regarding my stunned expression, he chuckles, showing his amusement.

"I can't believe you have this office all to yourself." The room is about ten times the size of my office at work and three staff share it quite comfortably. I also don't have a window the size of a Mack Truck on one wall, or space for a comfortable seating area separate from the obvious work space.

I approach the dark wood round table and run my fingers over it. The finish is perfection. Someone paid a hefty price for such amazing construction, and he's using it as a boardroom table. There are six chairs neatly tucked underneath it. One is a slight bit angled, so I fix it, out of habit. If there weren't black casters on the leather high-back chairs, it could have passed for a lovely dining table. I'd hate to slide anything but paper over such a lovely, rich wood.

Dustin's now seated behind his solid wood desk, looking strong, robust, and powerful. He tilts back in his chair, that smirk making me think naughty things, when I know he should be focusing on getting down to work. Instead he watches me move around his office, exploring the room and all his decorative treasures.

I turn to smile at Dustin, but forget instantly what I was going to say to him, paralyzed by the view. Dustin looks like a dark force, centered in the colorful picture window, with volatile storm clouds the moving picture behind him. We lock eyes from across the room. His face changes from thoughtful to menacing, a smirk molding onto his perfect, cupid bow lips.

Fighting off the desirous sensation now flooding every nerve ending in my body, I take a breath. "Don't you have work to do?" My sarcasm lashes out like a whip, but it doesn't affect the amused look on his face. He's determined, unwavering in his confidence.

"I like watching you appreciate the finer things in life. You have a good eye for detail."

"I have a good eye for many things, Mr. Miller, and if I'm correct, that means you're flirting with me." I make my way toward him, not shrinking beneath his full-bodied stare, the red shoes powering my advance. A feminine confidence is a dangerous thing, and I don't know how long I can keep it up, but when we're alone like this, I find myself with loose lips and a strong libido.

"Are you saying you don't like it when I look at you like this?" His chair squeaks when it returns upright, and he's on his feet, meeting me at the corner of his desk, like I've called him there urgently.

"No," I whisper, his lips now very close to mine, his hand slipping around the curve of my waist, guiding me closer toward him.

A smile quirks on his lips. "Good. Then I guess you won't mind if I do this." He leans closer, his other hand sliding around my shoulder and weaving into my hair, his lips interlocking with mine. The kiss is soft, in stark contrast to the grip he has on my hair. I feel how hard he's becoming in his pants, just from a kiss. When I buffer that hardness with my stomach, he doesn't shy away, accepting the rub of my softness against him.

He groans, deepening our kiss, drinking from my mouth like I'm flavored and delicious, his body twitching against me. The light scruff of his face from not shaving this morning scratches gently against my mouth, making me crave more of his touch. I don't want him to stop—ever.

His lips break free and he struggles for a breath, his voice coming low and husky. "You have no idea how hard it's been for me to keep my hands on top of your clothes; first, last night, and then this morning. You know I want you, right?"

I kiss him back, making up for all the times I'd wanted to earlier but didn't, for fear of rejection. "I never said you shouldn't." I barely pull back enough to speak, now feeling the pressure tightening between my hips.

When he moves, I move with him, his fingers pulling from my hair only to lift me into his arms. I wrap my legs around his waist. The sofa looks pretty comfortable and I expect him to drop me on there, but instead I find myself whirled in the opposite direction and flattened on a cool, hard surface. The table.

I lift myself up in time to watch Dustin unbuckling his belt. "What are you doing?" I flash a look out the window. "Someone might see you!"

"It's raining outside. An even bigger storm is coming. There's no one out there."

I swallow back the nerves balling up in the back of my throat, but my voice still sounds husky. "Someone might hear us?"

"Then I guess you better be very, very quiet." He drops his belt on the floor next to him, the click and thud echoing throughout the large, rectangular room. My entire body shudders. This is happening. He's actually going to do this here. With me.

Answering to my insecurities, he drops on top of me, the heaviness stealing the chill from my anxious body. He touches me, lifting my clothes to feel skin on skin, dominating my mouth and breaking through my lips with his tongue. I reach for his pants, but he saves me the trouble, his fingers working his zipper down quickly. I wriggle beneath him, my fingers clinging to the solid body hovering over me, wanting it all when I see, down the line of my body, that he has pulled himself free.

There are two quick knocks at the door. I freeze in place, but I see Dustin frantically refastening his pants. I hear the door handle twisting and am rolling off the table, shuffling across the floor, with disheveled panties. I push my skirt over my thighs, just as the woman peers inside, already talking.

She stops, abruptly. I stop where I am, my heart thudding in my ears, very few steps away from Dustin, hurried breaths held for the longest minute of my life.

"Oh, sorry," she finally blurts. "I didn't realize you had company." Most would turn and walk away, but not this girl. "I just have a few invoices I need approved. Do you mind?" She holds the papers out, with a pen extended to him, but she doesn't enter the room any farther than the doorway. She waits for him to say something. I realize it's because he hasn't invited her in.

"Yeah, uh, this isn't really a good time, Cindy." Dustin scratches the back of his head, like she walked in on an intense conversation, even with his belt at his feet and his hands clasped together in front of his crotch.

Still, the girl hesitates. Take the fucking hint! If I were more outspoken, I would say something, but I just wait in silent frustration for her to get a clue and show herself to the door. I hate myself for being so reticent, but I can't help it. I just stand there, like a deer in headlights, envious that she's stolen his attention even if only for one second.

Dustin doesn't say anything more, and he doesn't move to take the pen from her. The girl apologizes, realizing finally that he doesn't plan to help her out right now. She spins around and closes the door. *It's about time!*

Dustin leans forward and snatches up his belt, flashing a glance at me. "That was close."

I straighten myself, blushing under his fiery scrutiny, even now that the moment is ruined. Uneasiness has settled in, but it's right there, next to my anticipation. My body says one thing while my brain tells him *you're a bad, bad boy* for trying this at all.

"You think I should feel ashamed? Really, Izzabelle?"

A shiver wracks my entire body, reacting to the way he reads my body language. I want to answer him, but the way he prowls toward me prevents the breath from reaching my mouth. I turn for the door, but he beats me to it, backing me up until I have nowhere left to go but against it. He hovers over me, smiling wickedly, flattening his hands on either side of my head, until I'm captured between two muscular arms held stiff. His face moves intimately close to mine, a thin sheathing of air the only thing cushioning the space between us.

"What do you expect me to do with you sitting across the room looking all soft and coy? Your body speaks to me, Izzy. What do you think it says?"

He's asking me a silly question, so I give him an equally as useful answer. "I thought you came here to work . . . to do *other things.*" I really have no idea what he does exactly, but I never meant my comment to be taken sexually. The way my voice comes out, though, is breathy and seductive and that's exactly how he takes it.

"Things other than you?" His question hangs in the air between us. He saw the way I scowled at the girl who interrupted us and I can't deny that I liked having all that masculine attention on me.

"Yes," I say, again a mere breath, as he bends his elbows, moving even closer to me yet.

"That was the plan," he says, his breath rushing over my lips. "But you have an amazing way of making me want do *other* things." My body twitches when he presses the length of himself against me. "What are you doing to me, Izzabelle?"

The question is one I ask myself every day, dating back to the morning I woke next to him in my mother's guest bedroom. Guilt flickers over my face and I have to turn my eyes down so he can't see it manifesting there. This is all so new to me—having a man being so attentive toward me—but I have to wonder how many times his staff have found him in other compromising positions like this one. Deep in my heart, I doubt all of this is so new for him.

"Izzabelle, tell me what you were thinking just now." His voice is still rough, but the order is soft, like he's begging for me to say it.

He tilts his head sideways to meet my downturned eyes, but he doesn't remove his palms from the wall behind me. Even with his arms firmly seizing me in front of him, he somehow manages to will my eyes up to his. I hate having to admit my insecurities to him. The last thing I want to do is remind him how inexperienced in relationships I am.

My voice comes out calmly, my hands clenched in fists at my sides. "If you must know, I was thinking about how your staff are probably used to finding you in situations like this."

"What do you mean *like this*?"

He doesn't know how intimately he's pinning me right now? "Finding you with women in your office, doing less than business-like things." A red color burns across my cheeks like a flaming freight train. He puts a stop to my question in an instant.

"No, Izzabelle. I don't bring women to my office. I may

have fucked up in the past, but don't mistake me. This is a place of work. The only reason a woman has ever stepped foot in this building with me is out of necessity. For social gatherings. But only for show."

My heart feels like it's ready to explode, hearing him talk about being with other women, the thudding pulse tightening things in my chest. "That explains why you always take the busty blondes." I wish he wasn't so close to me when I said it, so I could blush without knowing he feels the heat rushing off my skin.

He smirks at me, but there's no humor in it. "I wonder myself why I have always chosen women like that. I mean, there's nothing wrong with long, beautiful legs." One of his hands drops down from the door and grazes up my naked thigh. "They always have their nails done and their faces painted." He glances down at my fisted hand and I keep it that way, so he can't see the way my nail polish is chipping.

"And that's what you like?" I ask, the sadness etching across my face.

Dustin sighs and stares into my eyes. "I guess. But I never see the real women hiding behind the masks. Except for you, Izzabelle. I always see the real you."

The rush of heat in my cheeks transforms into a rage, while I hear the word "different" ready to fall from his lips. I'm so tired of being the outcast. I shift in my heels and lift a flat gaze to meet his. "No, I don't wear much makeup. Thanks for pointing that out. You don't think I know that I look different from the women you prefer? I don't need you to rub it in my face, Dustin." I flatten my hands on his chest and try to push him away, but he remains unmoved, with a stern set to his eyebrows.

I give up quickly, my hands resting on his chest, waiting for him to back down, as the storm rages on just beyond the glass window. I see the way his jaw tenses near his ears when he clenches his teeth. Even though I hate admitting it—when I should be ripping him a new one—it's cute.

"I don't think you get it," he growls, like the rumble of thunder. There's a strength in his determination and the threat is intoxicating. I have to keep listening because my heart is contending for an Olympic race at the rate it pounds.

"Izzabelle—you—you are the woman I prefer. When I'm with those girls, they're always hiding behind that mask. The tan. The painted faces. Fake eyelashes. Do you think I like that? I know it's not them." He takes a loud breath and hits me with those eyes. "You know, maybe at one time I liked the feeling of being wanted by them, but the sensation is hollow when it's one-sided. No one *ever* opens up to me. Do you think I ever wanted them to?"

I think his question is rhetorical, but I get it. He wants to get to know me—not those busty bitches—me!

23

I've Got It Bad For You

I'm stunned by everything Dustin says and all that it means. I cling to a breath and dig my teeth into a smiling bottom lip, now that the rage has left my chest. My body softens against him, but his eyes drill into mine, surrounding me in darkness so that I only see him when he speaks.

"I've got it bad for you, Izzy. You know it. My dad knows it. The whole fucking club knows it. Never devalue yourself for being pure or different." The last of his words are a dark whisper, as his arms collapse around me.

I accept the soft press of his lips and the sharp lick of his tongue, writhing and whimpering from the sweet tension between my thighs. His fingers comb into my hair, holding my face firmly where he wants it to be while he woos me.

"I love the way you are, Izzy. I love that you can wake up in the morning, run a brush through your hair and look ready for the day. It's a miracle how little time you spend getting ready and you still look like you do. You are all the things I always hoped a woman could be, Izzy. You are everything I've never had."

I question him with a squint in my eyes. If I'm everything he's never had, then it makes me curious to know who he has had. Again, he answers me, so there's no question left in my face.

"Gold diggers," he says. "It's no secret I have money, and with a body like this—" His hand waves over himself, giving me a chance to pull away from the door, but I don't take it.

"I draw the wrong kind of girlfriend," he finally admits, like he's cursed to suffer from one casual fling to the next for the rest of his life.

"And me?" I say, outwardly cringing, wishing I hadn't asked such a stupid question.

He reaches his one hand out and presses it into the door behind me. "It's different. It's just different with you."

He tries to make it sound like it's a special kind of different, but I wonder if he only wants me because I'm off limits—forbidden. I'm not anything like he's used to and I'm pretty sure once our parents return, and my mom convinces his dad to give us their blessing, he won't feel the same way about me. I sink into my lower class, suddenly feeling like a sore thumb, in a club where I obviously don't belong, with a man a little too handsome for my standards.

I dive under his bicep, but he wraps his arms around my waist and spins me around until we're face to face again.

"When I'm with you, Izzabelle, I feel wanted in a way I've never been before. My body responds to every sensation passing through you like we are meant to be one. That shy look in your eye, the one you're giving me right now, tells me all I need to know about you. You may be wary about me, but you're honest. You'll never know how appreciative I am of your honesty."

My eyelashes flutter shut, my breaths coming raggedly. The heat from his body has suddenly blossomed, warming me like a natural fireplace on a cold winter night.

"Is it a sin for me to say these things, Izzabelle? I like the feeling I get when you're with me. I like having you by my side. Is it wrong for me to feel the way I do? Because it doesn't feel wrong—not to me. Not even a little bit. In fact, it feels a whole lot more right than anything else in my life these days."

My heart flutters from all the compliments and I can't even keep the shield there to protect myself from the fall that will inevitably come. I shake my head to acknowledge what he's said, giving him something, while I'm unable to come out with any words to express myself.

His arms tense around my waist. "If you want to be with me, and I mean more than just in my bed, then let's be. I don't care what my staff think, I don't care how the club guests think, and I really don't care how Rusty feels about it." He gazes down at me and it drives home his point. "You are the one with all the power here. If you want me, I'm yours. Just say the word, Izzy, and I'm yours."

Just say the word? What word? The heat coming off his body wraps around my shoulders and swallows me like a warm fleece blanket while he waits for an answer, but I don't know what word he's looking for! When I try to speak, my voice cracks. My throat is dry and I'm not even sure what I plan to say when I do speak.

All I know is that I want him—without a shadow of a doubt, I want him—and I can see it in his eyes that he knows this just from looking at me. A single tear escapes my eye and travels the slow path down my face. Dustin eyes that tear, but he doesn't comment until it drips off my chin and splatters on the floor.

"I am the reason for your tears," he finally says, like he's guilty of a horrendous crime.

It's true, he is responsible, but not in the way that he thinks. I wish I had the confidence to tell him exactly how I feel, but my nerves prevent me from saying that four letter word that I think he might be waiting for.

"Have I upset you?"

Rain pelts softly against the windows as the storm continues to mimic my emotions. I shake my head briskly, my hair tossing side to side. He has it all wrong.

Dustin's thumb trails slowly down the path of the tear, gently drying it up. "Right when I thought I knew how to read you, you come out with those tears and it rips me apart. It's hard for me to think clearly with these things hanging out here." He digs a tear out of the corner of my eye with his knuckle.

I slide my hands up his chest, feeling the firm muscles there. They flex and constrict beneath my fingers while I find my voice. "I think you know that I have feelings for you, but it goes farther than that—farther than I think I'm ready to admit. You—" I swallow. He's been so frank with me, I don't want to leave him with nothing. "You make me feel a way I've never had to explain out loud before, and that scares me."

With that small admission, the look of unsureness on his face clears and a smile replaces the flat expression that was once there. His body presses deeply into me, his hands gripping my ass, his mouth smoothing shamelessly over mine. He waits for a response from me, by way of whimper, before sinking in deeper to the exchange. I open my mouth to accept him, feeling like I myself am hopelessly sinking in deeper—deeper into a bottomless pit of love. There is no escape.

Our lips part naturally, our breaths synced together.

He smirks at me. "I'd love to spend the rest of my day doing just this, but since it doesn't look like I'm going to get any work done with you here, why don't we grab a bite to eat?"

"Okay," I agree, loving the way he steals one last kiss before pulling me into the public eye again. I catch another glimpse of the wet, colorful landscape on the other side of the window and notice a ray of sunshine breaking through the impossibly dark clouds, before being tugged away from the view.

Dustin escorts me through his club, smiling and nodding at all the staff and guests who pass us, my hand tucked against his side and enfolded in his. It looks like there's in-house dining and that's right where he's taking me.

"Don't laugh," he says as he pulls open the door with the same crest marking the glass that you'll find on every other branded item in the place.

I see what he's talking about. The restaurant is called *The Clubhouse*. "Real original," I say, with a smile.

He doesn't resist raising his eyebrows to show that he agrees, but he quickly turns forward to acknowledge the hostess. "I can show her to the table. Thank you, Angela," he says, skipping past the woman standing there with the big smile, but only after plucking the menus from her hand.

He pulls me through the dimly lit room of dark blacks, rich chocolates, and warm dinner conversation. There's so much to take in, while Dustin shows me to a seat near the panoramic window, a theme I've noticed throughout the entire north and rear side of the building. Our round table is draped in a long chocolate cloth as dark as his eyes, with crisp white plates, crystal goblets, and a fabric napkin adorned with the trademark logo for the Carver Mountain Country Club resting on top. There's a small cluster of fresh-cut flowers dangling from a smooth, clear vase in the center of the table—very chic and contemporary.

Dustin holds the dark wood chair for me—always a gentleman—tucking me under the edge of the table. Before he leaves my side, I place my hand on his forearm and lean close to speak with him privately. Every table is full, except for this one. How did he know it would be available to him? "The sign out front said *By Reservation Only*. I hope we aren't stealing someone's seat."

"Izzabelle, there are few things for you to worry about when you're with me, and troubling anyone in this club is not one of them. This table is permanently reserved for my father. Soon it will be mine. When it comes to seats in this house, you will always be the first offered one. Get used to it."

He pulls away, my hand sliding from his arm, but he doesn't go far. He takes the seat right next to me, so we're both glancing at the view, the entire clubhouse to our backs. Although I feel bad for the people with dinner reservations, who have to wait for a table, it's hard to fight with a man who feels so passionately about my contentment and wellbeing. I keep my mouth shut and show him how grateful I am for his hospitality, with a smile and easy conversation.

We both take the opportunity given to us to relax and unwind, with a single glass of wine, wandering touches, and a smile. It is a day I will long remember, after devouring the wonderful fresh foods delivered to our table. You'd think with such an amazing view outside that I would have memorized it, but my eyes never leave the man sitting next to me.

His chair is now pulled close to mine, and the waitress comes by yet again to ask whether we need anything else. Dustin doesn't even glance to our waitress when he answers her.

"That'll be all for tonight. Please put it on my tab. Thank you."

I can't stop smiling. He doesn't even give the young lady a friendly glance. He clasps his hand on top of mine, his touch making me shiver softly. His eyes are all for me. I think it's becoming pretty obvious that we both have everything we need right here. Where I thought our night would end, it's only just begun. The little bit of privacy doesn't go unappreciated, but I don't expect the conversation.

Dustin opens up his heart to me and I start to feel a sense of happiness that I've never felt in all my days. But it's not until he says this, "Rusty and I get everything," that I know he's taking me seriously as a girlfriend. For a man concerned about gold diggers trying to take his money, it means a lot that he would share that information with me. Trust. That's what we're building tonight.

"You don't have to tell me that. I don't care about your money." I say it because it's the truth.

His hand lands back on top of the table next to mine. I watch him examine my fingers as he links them between his. His hand is warm and big, a comforting thing that I enjoy very much.

"I know you don't care, but I want you to know." He looks up at me, holding my gaze. He's not done yet. "When my mom came back a few years ago, she tried to rip the country club out from underneath my dad." He glances over his shoulder, making sure no one can overhear what he's about to tell me. He leans in closer, everyone more than a table away mistaking our closeness for canoodling. "I was so afraid that he would give everything to her. She still had this uncanny hold over him, even then. I worried that if she caught him while he wasn't thinking too clearly, she might get what she asked for, but I was wrong."

"What do you mean?" I ask softly.

"Your mother married a smart man."

I smile at his compliment. "Obviously your dad is skilled in many areas. The country club didn't get to be this popular because of a brute attitude and heavy-handed management."

Dustin smirks at me. "My mom didn't know this, but you're about to. It killed her to learn that my dad had transferred his entire estate to Rusty and me the year Rusty turned eighteen. He also opened up a new LLC. Guess who the sole shareholders are."

My mouth drops open. "The club is yours?"

"On paper, yes, but we respect our dad and the chances he's taken for us. It's his until he's ready to walk away from it. But like I said, eventually, Rusty and I will get everything."

He pauses, a thoughtful expression passing over his face, before continuing. I notice the way he wears a hurt expression every time he speaks of his mother. I can't imagine the bullshit she's put him and his father through all these years.

"It wasn't until she tried to take him for all he's worth that she found out he's only worth the personal debts in his name and the few thousand dollars in his bank account."

I squeeze his hand to show him that I understand how hard it must have been for him to go through all that agony at such an ill-equipped age. My father has hassled my mother over the years and I saw the way it ate away at her every time he did it. Has he struggled with it the same way? It looks like it's taken a lot for him to admit this to me out loud. But, why?

"Why are you telling me this?"

"Because I want you to know what you're getting yourself into by letting yourself into my life. My mom isn't out of the picture, not by a long shot. Giving me a try is like opening a can of worms, and you don't get to decide what happens and when. She's like a loose cannon aimed directly at me. There's no saying what she'll do when she finds out that she's not the only woman in my life anymore."

I slide my hand under the sleeve of his short-sleeved shirt and over his bicep, enjoying the feel of his skin over the hard muscle. "It's a little late for me, isn't it?"

"I don't know, is it?"

We stare into each other's eyes and that's when I realize just how far gone I am. He knows it too.

"Dustin, is that you?" a woman shouts from across the dining room. It looks like a female employee. She's wearing the uniform. Is she really that shocked to find him in his own country club? She weaves around the tables to get a closer look.

I know I'm scowling at the blonde girl now, but so are the guests around me. She's just rude. Who does that in such an intimate setting? It's disrespectful and I give her my full opinion with narrowed eyes. It has nothing to do with how gorgeous she is, but I can't help but notice how good she looks with those long, straight bangs, as white as sand. Even with a pony tail on the back of her head, she looks dazzling. No one would ever accuse me of being dazzling.

Dustin holds up a hand to stop her from carrying on, and it silences her, but she still rushes to his side, pony tail bouncing.

"Lena told me I'd find you here. I thought you were busy," she says, like finding him has been a disappointing surprise.

His eyes flick over at her, making me wonder if he likes what he sees. She's everything he's always looked for in a woman in the past. Her foundation is seamless, making her look like she has flawless skin, and if I didn't look closely, I wouldn't have noticed that she had drawn on the shape of her full, pouting lips. Has he dated her before? The way she regards him, so casually, I know that has to be it.

"Do you have a minute?" she asks, her glance barely flickering toward me. She doesn't care what I think. She's asking him.

He doesn't look up at her, instead checking me over for a reaction as he says, "I'll be there in a minute." The firm order in his voice sends her slinking back to her post at the front of the room, like a scorned child, while my heart is ramming a new hole into my throat.

I try to keep my expression soft and unconcerned, but damn . . . I'm jealous! Why does he have to go see her? What could she possibly need from him? What could he possibly want from her?

I cling onto a breath, waiting for him to speak, to save me from all these crazy assumptions already!

He turns back to me, speaking softly, like this should be easy for me to understand. "You see what my life is about? There's always going to be work to do. There will always be someone dragging me away."

Work? Really? Are you sure that's all it is?

My imagination runs wild, but I force the anger down and answer softly. "It's okay."

I kick my foot out from under the long table dressing and glance at the extravagant thing strapped there. It catches Dustin's attention too, but staring at my feet isn't going to keep the emotion at bay. I can feel it swelling in my chest and raging upwards, like a Tsunami. I take a deep breath, before I allow it to sweep me away, attempting to regain some of the calm I'd enjoyed for the better part of the afternoon.

"Come with me?" Dustin asks, like the idea just comes to him. He clasps onto my hand, helping my decision along.

I swallow, gazing into his eyes for five long seconds. I find something there. He doesn't want me to hurt for him. *It's just for business.* "I won't be much help," I admit.

"You'll make my night brighter." He stands and holds his other hand out to help me to my feet. I slide out of my chair and give him my right hand. He waits for my approving smile before tugging me along next to him.

A phone call. That's all she needed him for. And here, I've been concocting all these horrible scenarios of why she might like to get him alone. While Dustin rushes back to his office to take the call, I excuse myself to use the ladies' room and then loiter outside the restaurant to call the mechanic about my car, leaning against a wall in the hallway.

"Hi, this is Izzabelle Spade. You brought my car in earlier today," I remind the mechanic, wondering why the hell I haven't heard from him all day.

"The car isn't ready yet."

That's all he's got? "What do you mean, it isn't ready?"

"We were waiting on a part and it just showed up, but it was quitting time half an hour ago. It'll have to wait until tomorrow."

I end the call, cringing. It sounds like I'll be spending another night at the Miller residence. I call my friend, Sadie, and ask her to stop by my mom's house to feed the cat.

"Use the key. It's in the same place as always . . . under the big pot next to the barbeque on the back porch. The food's in the kitchen cabinet next to the sink."

Sadie doesn't sound really impressed with me. I'll have to make it up to her. "I owe you big time."

She agrees. "Yeah, you do. Have a good time, though."

"Okay, I gotta go. Talk to you later."

She ends the call just as I find my way back to Dustin's office. I knock on his door before entering. He's the only one there, waving for me to come in and take a seat. The sky is so black, all I see is my reflection in the long window behind him as I walk toward him—that and a few dim lights on the golf course in the distance.

I wait patiently for him to finish the call, loving the way he works his jaw during his negotiation, his eyebrows rising and falling over his eyes as he listens to the offer.

"You've got yourself a deal. Have your attorney send over the contract." He glances up at me and smiles. "I look forward to doing business with you."

He hangs up his phone and stares into my eyes, looking really happy to see me. "I did it. My dad is going to be so happy to hear this news. Shit, this calls for a celebration. I'm going to get a bottle of the best from the basement cellar. I don't suppose you want to come with."

Smirking at him, I answer. "Not really. Spiders and dark, narrow spaces aren't really my thing."

"It's not all that small, to be honest. The Millers don't do anything small. But, yeah, I'd be lying if I told you there aren't any spiders."

I scrunch my lips and he chuckles at me, getting out of his chair and walking toward me. A flicker of déjà vu has my body temperature rising. He smirks at me, thinking the same thing.

His fingers sweep over my cheek. "I won't be long. But I am expecting a call on my dad's line. Would you mind answering it if it rings? I'll be five minutes tops."

"Okay."

He points at a button on the phone. "Lift the receiver and hit the group pick up button. It's as easy as that."

"I can do that."

He kisses my cheek and heads for the door, smiling back at me. "I won't be long."

The door clicks shut and I instantly get to my feet and run my fingers along his desk as I stroll around it. Not two seconds after I settle back in his big boy chair, the phone rings. My eyes frantically search the keys for the group pick up button. I lift the receiver, my finger running over the display until I find it. I press the button, but don't think twice about what I am going to say when I do.

"Hello?" I slap my hand over my eyes, embarrassed about my substandard greeting.

"Who is this?" It's a woman, and she's snapping at me. Why would a woman who sounds invested in Jason's visitors be calling for him?

"This is Izzabelle, on behalf of Dustin Miller. He'll only be a minute. Would you care to hold for him?"

An evil cackle encompasses my ears. "Oh, you must be one of the new whores putting my boys in the headlines. Thank you for that, by the way."

A confused expression takes its time passing over my face. "What are you talking about?"

The woman is very happy with herself and I don't buy the innocent change in her tone at all. "Today's newspaper. Oh, I'm sorry, hun. Haven't you seen it yet? Have a look and let me know how I did."

I don't understand what she's babbling on about. "You must have the wrong number. This is the office of Dustin Miller. I only answered his phone for him. You must have me confused with someone else."

"Oh, no, sweetheart. This is the right number, I assure you, and you are exactly who I think you are."

I should probably hang up the phone. This woman sounds like the devil herself. But I find myself wanting to pry, with more questions. "You're calling for Jason?"

"You got it," she says. "I'm calling to collect what's mine."

"You and Jason, you're close?"

"You could say that," she answers.

I let out a small laugh. "Then why would you be calling for him while he's on his honeymoon." As soon as I feed her the line, I realize the folly to my plan. I screwed up. No one's supposed to know about Jason's plans—not the wedding and not the honeymoon—not with the local media hounding everyone for information. I knew that. I let my guard down, and now I am royally screwed.

"I should have guessed as much. Where did the bastard take her?"

It's too late now. What's been said has been said. I can't take it back now. But I'm not that dumb. I won't be falling for that one. "Somewhere nice, I'm sure."

"Oh, snappy. Maybe you're not the pushover they're talking about in the news, after all."

"What do you want?"

"First, you should be asking who I am."

I roll my eyes. "Who are you?" But I already know who she is: Cruella de Vil.

"I'm Janey, Dustin's mother dearest, but you can just call me Mom."

"Yeah, I don't think so."

"Aww, that's too bad. I was hoping we could be friends."

"You're no friend of mine. What do you want, Janey?"

"Good girl. You should probably get to the point before Dustin returns to his office. I'd hate for him to walk in on our little conversation."

My eyes flash around the dark room, looking for someone to jump out of the shadows in the corners, but no one does. My eyes blaze out the back window into the darkness, while she continues to taunt me. Is there someone out there watching me? I can feel her eyes on me, like an icy finger licking up my spine.

"I doubt Dustin's told you just how lucky you are to have snared him. As I'm sure you've guessed, he's wealthy. But did you know he's in line to get a healthy family fortune? My fortune," she snaps, her voice turning cold and heartless. "But you don't have to wait for Jason to die for Dustin to get everything. It's already his."

I squint into the darkness, wondering why this stunned bitch is sticking her nose where it doesn't belong. "Why are you telling me this?"

"It's what you wanted to hear, isn't it?"

"No." My voice comes out harshly and it tickles her pink. I want to smash the phone down and break it into a million pieces, but I know that won't harm her one bit.

"Tell me you didn't already know this."

"That's none of your business." I try to maintain my cool, but the flat tone doesn't trick her.

"Wow. He must really trust you if he's already telling you all his secrets. It'd be a shame for the media to get a hold of this one."

I scowl out the window, through my own reflection. "You wouldn't."

"Don't scowl dear, it'll give you wrinkles."

I drop the phone when I shuffle to my feet, and the receiver hits the speaker button as I back away from the window.

"Quit being so dramatic," Janey says, her voice pouring over Dustin's office, echoing loudly. "Of course not. He's my son. I wouldn't do anything to harm him. What kind of woman do you take me for?"

A sense of relief rushes me, but it's short-lived. I know this woman cannot be trusted. My eyes flicker impatiently to the door, like I'm waiting to get caught in this predicament. I know Dustin is not going to be happy with me. I rush back to the phone. "I'm hanging up now," I tell her. No good will come of prolonging this conversation.

"Oh, Izzabelle. One last thing," her voice booms. "You speak none of this to Dustin. If I get even one small hint that he knows about our little chat tonight, our one-on-one interview will go live, and I have a feeling he won't like you very much after that."

A sickening sensation fills my stomach when I hear the replay of my voice repeating the words I never meant to share in the first place, "... *he's on his honeymoon.*"

"Where did you say Jason was?" she says to me, imposing my voice into her one-sided conversation.

... he's on his honeymoon.

And she's already edited it to make it sound like our discussion was candid.

He must really trust you.

Yeah, I don't think so.

I'm speechless, but Janey isn't.

"What would you say if I asked you whether you think Jason's marriage will last?"

Before I'm given a second to answer, I hear my voice again.

No.

The harshness of my voice kills me. The way she strings my words together, makes it sounds like I hate Jason and I'm only after Dustin for his money. "You can't do this," I state carefully, although inside I'm screaming at the top of my lungs.

"Oh, sweetie, I already have."

"You'll never get away with this."

"Is that right?" She's so wickedly confident. "Tell Dustin about this and everyone will know just how greatly you dislike your new stepdaddy. How do you think that will make Sarah feel?"

"Leave my mother out of this."

Janey ignores me completely, like she's lost in her own little world. "Dustin might get over it, eventually, but that remains to be seen. Should I send it for production?"

She's threatening me with the only thing that matters to me—love. My loose lips have put my entire family at risk. If I tell Dustin about this, the whole city will be up in arms about it. The media will drive a stake through me and there'll be no chance at a private relationship with Dustin after that.

Everyone's been so supportive of Jason finding love. The media has tried to paint him in a dark light, but the attention has backfired. They love him. They want more.

I refuse to be the one to give them more. "No. This discussion will never leave this room."

"You're going to have to do better than that, my dear."

I second-guess my decision, but the interview sounds so real. Even if I told my mom it was a hoax, would she believe me? If I tell Dustin in secret what Janey has planned, will he trust that it's a trick? I'm afraid this is all it'll take for Dustin to put me in my place, with all his other untrustworthy exes. I've made my decision.

"I won't tell him."

That sickening laugh of hers slides over my shoulders, a disgusting feeling resonating in my gut. "Good girl. Now see to it that he never finds out or our friendly little chat goes public."

A rage washes over me. She has all the power. I want to scream, but I know she's somehow watching me. I turn away from the glass so she can't see the play of emotions in my eyes. I know she'd find a way to turn even that against me. The call ends while I'm thinking about what kind of threat I want to serve her.

"Hello?" I say, but there's no response. I turn and glance at the phone, one second passing like an hour. I replace the receiver and push away from the desk, getting as far away from that voice as humanly possible.

I've barely even caught my breath by the time Dustin returns to the room. He's still in a joyous mood and even in the circumstances, when he whisks me around him, toting a bottle of bubbly, it makes me smile.

"Hey, everything okay?"

I nod my head, unwilling to lie to him.

Suddenly, the phone rings. My eyes burst out of their sockets, but he releases me before he notices anything out of the ordinary. He puts down the bottle and reaches across his desk to pick up the call. My heart races in my chest, beating in my ears, deafening me like a bass pounding, volume cranked to the top. A ball of vomit lodges in the back of my throat as I watch him speaking into the phone. I can't hear a word of it. It's not until he's hugging me back into his arms that I come to.

"What's wrong?"

"I'm not feeling so well."

"I hope you're not sick."

He lifts me into his arms and I roll into his chest, with my cell phone clutched in my trembling hand. He leaves the bottle on his desk. "We can celebrate another time. I'll send Rusty down to the mechanic's to get your car."

This ruse would explain my hotter than hot face and short conversation, but how long can I keep it up before the guilt breaks free? My voice is quiet. "It's not ready."

"Okay, I'll get you back to your place then. I doubt you'll find any comfort in my bed. You probably want to get back home."

Oh, but he's wrong. I realize now, I'll have to change things up if I plan to spend the night at his place. I kick my feet, until he puts me down. "It's okay, I can walk."

He takes my hand and we walk quickly down the hall, past the lobby and toward the back entrance where we'd come in hours earlier.

"My purse!" I just now realize I've forgotten it somewhere, but where? My nerves have my stomach rolling like a heavy thunder, as I run through our afternoon, thinking about the moment I last had it.

"I can't remember bringing it back to your office after dinner."

"The clubhouse." He shows me the way.

The foot traffic in the dark restaurant has slowed, but there are still a decent number of tables filled for late-night dinner conversation. We shuffle between the tables and I rush forward, dropping to my knees when I see it sitting next to my chair. Hugging it to my chest, Dustin pulls me to my feet.

"Check it," he tells me.

"I'm sure it's fine."

"Check anyways. I know the guests here don't need the money, but it doesn't mean there aren't ulterior motives for nosing through your things."

I flip through my wallet, but don't see anything missing, not even the twenty dollar bills. Everything seems to be in order. I shake my head with a look that suggests everything is as it should be.

"Come on," he says, like he knows something is wrong.

We walk silently to his car, but the way his eyes scatter the lot tells me he knows we're being watched, too. He gets my door, but leaves me to close it. I snap my own seatbelt and stare out the window. An eerie sensation comes creeping in, giving me the chills. I know someone's out there, but they're good at what they do. I scan the parking lot again, but I don't see anyone.

Someone is definitely watching us, though, and I don't think going home tonight is the right answer. I'm not going home tonight. But I also can't tell Dustin why—not until I figure out what the hell is going on here.

24

What's for Dessert?

Dustin takes me back to his place. I convince him that watching a movie might help. We watch it with Rusty, and I'm silent throughout the entire thing. Of all movies to pick, it's a horror one that leaves me on edge, checking the shadows for the boogie man. Dustin finds it hilarious and takes advantage of my nerves by wrapping me in his arms and holding me close.

"I got you. There's nothing you need to worry about," he says.

But that's just not true.

I like cuddling against him. I feel protected in his arms. But I'm afraid when he finds out what I've done that there will be no more friendly exchanges between us. Would telling him fix that?

No. If I tell him, this little thing we have going on here is over.

"Well. I think I'm going to call it a night," Rusty says, groaning when he stretches his arms toward the ceiling.

My soft smiles and the way I've been nuzzling against Dustin has him oblivious to the real reason for my unease. Soon, Rusty is gone, and I'm being lead back to Dustin's bedroom.

"It looks like you'll be spending another night in my bed."

I love the sound of that, but when he gives me a kiss and pulls the pillow back down from the closet, I realize he's going to try and pull his gentleman stunt again. The blinds are closed completely, but if he thinks I'm sleeping in here alone again, he's got another thing coming. I reach for the door and push the button in the middle of the handle, walking back toward the bed with a swagger.

Dustin has a look at me and catches me smiling wickedly. That's because tonight *I won't be sleeping alone.* "We've had another long day," he says.

I strip my shirt off, flaunting my average-sized breasts in the best push up bra the market has to offer. He's watching, but he doesn't move from the closet doorway, and he doesn't make eye contact with me. I slip the rest of my clothes to the floor, my skirt going first, and then my thigh highs, and then my bra.

"What are you doing?" he asks me, knowing damn well what I want here. And with his eyes planted on my bent-over form, I know I'm going to get what I want.

I climb onto his bed, wearing nothing but my panties and a smile, knowing he loves the way my ass weeble-wobbles as I get to the middle of it. I turn around and meet his heated stare. He licks his lips, battling with an inner argument I can't hear, but I can see the difficulty marring his strong, masculine features. He doesn't want to come any closer to me, but that is just not going to work for me tonight.

"Dusty, will you get over here already?"

He rips off his belt and paces across the floor, climbing over me, our mouths crashing into each other. Our bodies collide in a wave of unrequited desire, his fingers digging into my hair. My hands slip in between us to unbutton his shirt. I need to slide my hands up that warm, hard chest, see that smooth muscle playing beneath my fingers.

I slide his shirt over his shoulders, pinning his arms at his sides until he yanks free from it and tosses it haphazardly onto the floor. He kisses me harder, responding to my pleas, his well-kissed lips shocked when I climb over his lap and force him onto his back. My hands explore every rigid muscle down the front of him, paying special attention to the tight one in his pants.

He smiles, warning me with a deep growl. "You little

vixen. I was trying to be a gentleman."

I give up on his pants when I realize I'm not going to get into them on my own. "And you did a wonderful job for one night. Now I need you to act on your impulses and show me how badly you want me."

My mouth grows dry as he takes his time prying the button on his pants open. The anticipation is killing me. Everything feels new and exciting. I feel completely bared to him with the lights on, but I need him to be bared to me. He loses his pants soon after I tug on his waistband, his erection surging forward.

He rolls me onto my back, dropping his shorts in the process. I'm going to get it now, my body tightening with need.

"This wasn't supposed to happen," he growls, but there's no turning back now.

I sink back into his bed, fling off my panties and spread my legs wider. His manhood accepts my invitation, bouncing in approval. I gasp for a hurried breath as he slides over me, skin on skin.

I almost cry out from the extreme sensation. "That feels so good," I breathe.

He sighs with agreement, but feels the need to explain his surrender. "I wanted to give you tonight."

"Yes, I want you to give me tonight."

He chuckles. "Izzy, you're insatiable. I meant give you another night to think about us being together; make sure you want something more than this with me."

"I'm thinking about us being together right now," I answer, smirking, little else on my mind at the moment. I can't help it. He has me so horny all of a sudden, that I'm like a teenaged girl with a hard crush and no means of release. I need him to take me and rid me of the uncomfortable need overwhelming my body. If it were to shake the horrid sensation settling on the outskirts of my mind, even now, that would be a bonus.

"That's not exactly what I meant, Izzy. I need it to be more than night after passionate night." He slides over me again, in direct violation of his words. It's hard to think about anything but sex with the taunt of his rigid erection and the way his hard body hovers over me, but I'll give him whatever he wants at this point.

"If we do this, I'm taking my sweet old time," he says. "I will shower every inch of your body with *love*. No rushing it. If you want me to fuck you tonight, you're out of luck because I plan to make love to you, and when you climax, you will be all mine."

Guilt creeps into my heart—for making Dustin do this when he clearly had something more thoughtful in mind, and the fact that I'm keeping a dangerous secret from him doesn't help the situation. Would he do this if he knew?

He doesn't ask the tough questions, answering instead with soft, forgiving lips that tantalize my entire body until I'm seizing with pleasure.

He continues to touch me as his lips sprinkle kisses all over my neck and behind my ear. "I don't suppose you're on birth control," he breathes.

"No."

"Then we had better make this good."

I squint at him when he backs away, because I don't understand.

"I'm all out of condoms, Izzy. Like I said, I didn't plan on taking you home with me. I wanted to be sure this was going to work before we took things to this stage. Just remember, you're stuck with me. Even if this doesn't work, you're stuck with me."

His words don't dim the response of my body when he slides over me again. "I was going to respect your space and give you all the time you need."

My voice is shaky, but my point is true. "I've had enough space."

He shakes his head, as if I'm a naughty, naughty girl, and then reaches into his drawer and pulls out the last condom. He drops it on the bed next to me and leans forward, latching onto my breast like a hungry infant. My fingers sink into his hair when he moves to my other nipple, his body swelling back to its raging rigidity, as his manhood touches me where I've been begging him to ever since I shut the door.

An orgasm hits me out of nowhere, ripping from my body, with nothing but the press of his hardness on me. Gasping for a breath, my hands grope the strong v of his back, ending at a narrow muscled waist, with not a six, but an eight pack. His muscles flex, as I run my fingers over them. I open my mouth to draw air into my starved lungs, watching the way a certain part of his body grows larger than I thought possible. I want it, but he has other plans for me, licking, sucking and kissing me from head to toe.

Dustin's already proved just how patient and thorough a lover he can be. I get it, he's superman. His soft lips, pleasant tongue, and strong hands do things to me that I can't explain. I don't think I've ever climaxed this many times in one night. Okay, I know I haven't. But there's one act that I have been waiting ever so patiently for, and his loving is a major tease that I am ready to put an end to.

We exchange wistful smiles, but a trail of kisses down my stomach has me quivering with need. Dustin reaches for the condom, rips open the packet and rolls it on.

"I want to be inside you."

Finally! "Yes," I breathe. *That's what I want too!*

He hovers above me, settling on his forearms and sliding against me where I want him to be. The combination of such force and my sensitivity has me shouting out with ecstasy, and he hasn't even entered me yet. I clutch onto his forearms, bucking against him, watching the way he smirks, feeding off the desire in my eyes.

"You need me like I need you," he says gruffly, fighting his own need to take me quickly.

I slide my hands up and down the strong muscles of his back and grab onto a pair of solid ass cheeks. I spread my knees wider apart to accommodate him, knowing how tightly he's going to fill me with that extra-large cock of his.

He penetrates me slowly, and I dig my nails into his skin, so I don't scream. He groans as he slides a little deeper. My body involuntarily clenches and releases, as he continues to ease in, with a thickness that will surely break me.

"Look at me," Dustin insists. I didn't even realize that I was squeezing my eyes shut.

It's hard, but I manage to look at him through hooded luminous eyes.

"I love this." He leans in and takes my mouth, in a series of kisses that steals my breath away. He moves inside me, sharing rigid breaths between kisses, his stroke slow and steady, like the grip he has on my body.

I feel another orgasm building. Is that even humanly possible? But the tension is there, and I feel it tightening around him, preparing for the grand finale.

"I want to watch you," he says, and that only brings me closer, faster.

He hooks my legs over his hips and pulls me on top of him, so we're both sitting up, facing each other, my hands on his shoulders, his on my ass. He lifts me up, pulling me toward him, again and again, getting into a rhythm that has me whimpering louder with every thrust.

The closer I get, the harder he spears me, forcing himself in and out of my body. Every time he penetrates me, my pussy tightens around him. He moves faster and faster, until the speed of our ragged breaths sync together.

"Don't stop," I plead.

Dustin can't take it. He needs more control, and I let him have it. He flattens me on the bed and pushes into me, slowly, like I wasn't just about to finish again. Our eyes connect. A wicked grin appears on his face, as he exits my body and pushes back into place.

"This is making love?" I mock, cruelly begging him to finish me off.

His eyes narrow as he dips down to steal my mouth and possess my body with a hug that molds us into one. I pant for air, exchanging breaths with him as he hits the sweet spot with the depth of a single plunge, delivering me into a spiraling abyss of rainbows and sunshine.

I bury my back into the bed as he stiffens over me and

freezes in place. We both release a held breath at once, as he gives me all of him and then rests his moist forehead against mine.

"That," I whisper, running my fingers through the trace of hair regrouping across his chest.

"Incredible," he agrees, kissing me.

I don't remember much after that. We tangle in each other's arms and kiss late into the morning hours. Everything feels so surreal.

I awaken with a smile on my face. Dustin is in the bed next to me. He's wearing boxer shorts, but I am completely nude. A blanket is draped across my body, but one breast is exposed. The second Dustin notices this, his warm, rough hand closes over it. I moan with pleasure. He leans over me and gives me a kiss.

"Good morning."

"'Morning," I reply, stretching out next to him.

"Hungry for breakfast?"

I smirk. "I could eat."

"You pull some clothes on and I'll make you something."

"Mmmkay," I answer, watching him pull on a pair of jeans over a massive morning woody. His pants are so tight, he has to leave the top button undone.

My body sparks alive while I watch his fine ass leave the room. As his door clicks shut, sense returns to me. I roll out of the bed and stare at my wrinkled skirt on the floor. I don't exactly have anything with me to pull on. I left my overnight bag in my car.

I tiptoe across the room, clutching the sheet around my body, to peek in Dustin's top drawer, hoping to find a T-shirt. I find one, but when I look down at myself, after pulling it on, I see it's rather see-through.

Perfect.

I saunter out to the kitchen, where I find Dustin slaving over a modern stove. "Grab a seat," he says, without getting a good look at me. "It'll be ready in a minute."

The countertop is a mess. He's obviously trying really hard to impress me, rushing through the preparation; I let him do his thing, admiring the way his back flexes whenever he moves.

"What can I get you to drink?" When he glances at me—I mean, really glances at me—I almost wet my non-existent panties.

Dustin's wearing black rimmed glasses. And. He's. Wearing. Them. Right.

"Izzy?" he asks, not knowing what hit me.

He looks good—the frickin' man of my dreams!

"Orange juice. Orange juice would be great."

Within minutes there are two glasses of juice on the sturdy dining table and Dustin's dropping a large plate of chocolate chip pancakes in between us, with a dish towel thrown over his bare shoulder.

"Help yourself," he says, laying out a clean plate for me.

And I do, stacking two very large pancakes on my plate and drenching them in syrup. Dustin takes a seat across from me and watches me take the first taste. The pancakes are warm and moist, and the chocolate is mostly melted, but the centers are still slightly crunchy.

"Mmm. These are so good."

"You really think so?"

I would never lie about something so simple. "Yes. Yum!" I swallow another healthy bite. And the fact that he made them for me makes them that much more tasty. "You cooking. Very sexy, Dustin. Points all around."

He devours his plate of food with a smile and clears his end of the table, but not until he licks his fingers. My insides tighten with every digit he sucks clean, like his mouth is directly attached to my sensitive parts. Dustin appears beside me, with my head still in the clouds.

"More juice?" he asks, lifting my empty glass from the table.

"No. I'm good."

He drops my dishes into the sink and returns next to me, just then noticing what I'm wearing. His eyes linger on my chest, noticing the way my breasts press against the white fabric. "Whose is that?" he asks, curiously referring to my choice of clothes.

I look down at myself, knowing exactly what it'll do to him when I lift my chest up. I don't seem to have spilled anything, so he must be referring to the shirt itself. I look back up at him and smirk, smartly. "Oh, I don't know."

He so knows it's his.

"Izzabelle, please tell me you're wearing underwear." He growls like a dangerous animal.

"You want me to lie?" I lick the last of my syrup from my fork, which I realize I've been holding this entire time, and then place it on the table next to the leftover pancakes.

"Izzabelle. Are. You. Wearing. Underwear?"

My voice teases him seductively. "Why don't you come a little closer and find out?"

He prowls closer and glances at the half-emptied plate in the middle of the table. "Are you done here?"

"Yes."

He swipes an arm across the table, sending the plate and my fork clattering to the ceramic floor. I turn to face him, stunned and yet turned on by the fierce urgency to get me on my back. He picks me up and sits me where my plate last rested. I lean backwards and settle my palms on the table, with a front row view of Dustin and that sexy body.

He settles between my thighs, unzips his jeans and lifts the white T-shirt over my hips, exposing my privates, just as Rusty bursts out of his bedroom like the house is on fire. He's half asleep, but it doesn't take him long to figure out what's happening. Still, he asks, "What's going on out here?"

It's pretty clear we're about to get it on, and my aching pussy is exposed to a very erect Dustin.

"Dustin?" he asks.

But Dustin doesn't answer.

"Izzy?"

I don't look away from Dustin when I answer. "Everything is fine. Go back to your bedroom and close the door, please."

Dustin smirks, loving the fact that I don't move a muscle. *Oh, this isn't over yet.*

"Ah, fuck," Rusty shouts. "I'll be in the shower. You've got ten minutes."

He turns as Dustin mocks him. "Give us fifteen."

Rusty slams his door shut and Dustin's smirk turns even more mischievous.

I sit back up, nerves fluttering in my stomach. "What are you smirking at?"

"I'm ready for the next course." He lifts my T-shirt so it's propped just above my breasts, his big, warm palm flattening over my stomach and moving downwards, until he's smoothing over that place between my thighs.

"You dirty little slut," he says with a gravelly voice, when he finds me wet and ready.

He lifts my feet until they're resting on the table right next to my ass. Air rushes into my lungs when I gasp, because Dustin's pulling up my chair and having a seat, like he's preparing for a great feast.

"Lie back," he orders.

Before my hands hit the table, his mouth is closing around me. His moan vibrates through my pussy as he licks me with his tongue and feasts on me, his hands curling under my ass to pull me harshly against him, getting in there real good as I moan, my voice echoing through the kitchen.

He breaks free from my body, begging me to stop whimpering. "I'm all out of condoms, Izzy, and you're making me want to do something we're both going to regret."

My head is rolling side to side on the table, writhing with anticipation. I would love nothing more than to feel him inside me, skin on skin, but if he insists on protection . . .

"Rusty?" I suggest.

"He doesn't exactly carry my size."

My insides tighten and he watches the way I bite my bottom lip. "Dustin, please."

I need him, now.

He spins me around, answering to my pleas, and flattens my breasts to the table top.

"What do you want from me?" he asks. "Your pussy is strictly off limits."

I can't believe I'm saying this, but I want him that bad. "I have other holes."

His hands massage my ass cheeks, squeezing and spreading them. He wants to.

"You don't know what you're asking for." He strokes himself in front of me, staring at my spread legs. "I'll hurt you."

He leans forward and licks me, a full on lick. My entire body convulses.

"What did you do?" I gasp, stunned by the sudden act.

"I licked you."

"My ass!" I bark.

"Lubrication," he insists, rubbing himself over me.

"Don't do that again," I warn him, even though I war with how amazing it felt.

"I'm not going to enter you. You're going to have to make the first move."

I take two deep breaths, because I don't exactly know what I'm doing here and I'm sure it's going to hurt, but when his fingers find my pussy, my determination is renewed. Holding onto me with his left hand, he stokes himself with his right and presses against me.

"Have you ever done this before?" he asks.

My legs are shaking like a leaf. "Not exactly, but I've done a little reading, and they seem to really enjoy it in the porno flicks."

A blush rushes over my entire body, but he hardens against me, washing that embarrassed feeling away.

"It can be very pleasurable for a woman, but it can take some getting used to with a man of my size."

I take a deep breath and relax all my muscles. I'm a ball of nerves and excitement and a ring of anxiety envelopes me as I impale myself with his huge cock. I'm not going to lie: it fucking hurts! The reason I cry out is because it feels like he's ripping me a new one, but the way his fingers circle vigorously on my clit have me walking the tightrope between immense pain and extreme pleasure.

"If you back up farther, it won't hurt as much."

"Okay, okay, okay," I shout, easing back against him, if only to get more comfortable.

I force a relaxed breath. It takes me a second but I find a serene place where it doesn't quite hurt, it might actually feel good—really fucking good. He continues to touch me.

"Move," I plead.

"I'm not moving. I'll hurt you." Dustin remains frozen in place, while his cock twitches with rigour.

"Do it," I tell him.

"Are you sure you're ready?" He pulls back slowly.

"Move!" I order him, on the brink of discomfort.

He slams into me, bringing tears to my eyes, as Rusty reappears in his door.

Dustin remains locked inside of my tight body, while Rusty stumbles forward, having a hard time putting his tongue back in his mouth.

"Rusty," I scream. "What the fuck?"

"We're a little busy here. Some privacy?" Dustin suggests, because clearly Rusty can't think for himself at the moment.

We're both staring at him when Rusty flashes another look at my bare ass before returning to his room like he hadn't just caught us fucking on his kitchen table. A growling sound rumbles low in Dustin's throat. His hands slide over my ass cheeks and his erection hardens. It takes me a second to readjust to the large size. I lift my body up to try and get back to that comfortable position. It's not until Dustin puts his hands on me again that I find it.

His fingers resume their assault on my clit, while his other hand cups and massages my left breast.

"Do you still want this?" he asks, as I slide back against him, taking him one inch at a time.

He stiffens and I screech in a mix of torture and ecstasy that sends me right over the cliff, nosediving, head first into a pool of sexual stupor right behind him. That sensation sticks with me, even after his fingers stop moving. He doesn't budge and just relishes the feeling, having set my body off like an explosion, his warm breath on my neck and his arms around me holding our bodies together.

25

Home Sweet Home?

Having breakfast at the table Dustin had just exploited me on was a tad bit unusual, but it's the newspaper Rusty tosses in between us a minute after he retrieves it from the front porch that has my stomach in knots.

"I don't suppose you've seen this," he says, staring directly at his brother. The fact that he won't look at me says a lot. I brace myself for the worst, Dustin reading the headline and then digging in a little deeper into the article.

I see the moment when he starts to believe the lies. He turns dangerously dark eyes on me. "You spoke to my mother?"

"I didn't know," I answer quickly.

"Was that before or after I told you how she's out to ruin my life?" I see the hurt transform into anger and the anger turn into a disgusted wrath.

"Dustin, please. It was a mistake. I didn't mean for anyone to get hurt."

His eyes narrow and strike me like an arrow to my heart. "You do realize my mother owns the local newspaper."

"It's all right there, in black and white," Rusty adds, insulting me without explaining his words.

Tears rush to my eyes, but my curiosity refuses to let them fall.

Dustin's anger gets the best of him, but he reads a little more, before shifting into a monster. "What the fuck, Izzabelle?" his voice booms. "Use your fucking brain."

I twist away from that harsh stare and stomp toward the

door. He believes it—every word, without a second of thought that maybe his mother is lying, even just a little bit. "I think this is the first time I've used my brain since I met you," I screech, letting my inner bitch rear her ugly head.

I snatch my purse from his bedroom, pull on my shoes in a half-assed fashion and slam the front door before he's even left his seat at the table. I'm scrambling down the road in the shitty weather toward the mechanic's when Dustin appears on his porch, but I refuse to look back at him. "Izzabelle, wait!" He's sock-foot again, but the pavement is wet and this time he doesn't risk wet socks.

Without turning back, I shoot him the finger and hold it there for a good long minute so he knows exactly what I'm saying. I think he understands sign language too, because he doesn't speak again.

Sometimes when emotions run high, we say things we shouldn't. That's not the case here. He's an asshole. If he believes his mother over me, he's an asshole. If he truly believes I would ever set out to hurt him, or Rusty, or anyone in his family, even the bitch who started this all, then he's an asshole and I don't want anything to do with him.

Ten minutes later, I'm standing in the body shop, waiting for the mechanic to ring up my bill. At nearly a thousand bucks, I'm not happy, but I would never expect what happens next.

Declined.

I know my MasterCard is good for the money, but whatever. It must be his cheap-ass machine. "Here. Try this one." I hand him another card and I know this one is good, with a limit of five thousand dollars and not a penny spent on it.

Declined.

What. The. Ever-living. Fuck?

I look for a check, but realize now—of all times—that they're missing. I peek at the cash where I find three crisp twenty dollar bills. I offer them to the slimy man.

"That's not going to cut it, missy. You're going to have to

do a lot better than that if you plan to take that car out of here today." His greedy eyes work me up and down. "There are other methods of payment, if you know what I mean." The disgusting way he humps at the air makes me gag. I would never get on my knees for a dollar. I can't believe this piece of trash.

I snatch my money out of his hand, before spinning around and walking as quickly as humanly possible out of that building. My legs become wobbly and I shake violently from the distress, as I hustle out of the parking lot. Walking quickly is next to impossible in these shoes. I make it out of sight from the mechanic's shop, but I stumble on the wet sidewalk, crashing onto my knees, ripping my thigh highs and bloodying the pavement. I close my eyes and sigh. I will not cry. I will not cry.

Can my day get any worse?

My mother is out of the country. Sadie is an hour away. And I can't ask Dustin or Rusty for a penny after the accusations they were throwing at me. I'm up shit creek without a paddle. What am I supposed to do now?

I lift my eyes to find a bus stop not far up the road. It's like the light at the end of the tunnel. I climb to my feet and lift my chin, ignoring my bloody knees and scuffed shoes, limping all the way to the shelter. I purchase a ticket when the bus arrives, with the cash in my wallet. I don't think I had enough money to make it home, but the driver takes the bills and waves for me to get on anyway.

People stare at me, as I search for a seat. You think I don't know that I look like a natural disaster? I'm thankful to find an empty spot without a neighbor. The bus starts to move and the people continue to gawk, but no one asks me if I'm okay. I wouldn't know what to say if they had.

Within ten minutes, I'm assessing my knees and looking over my purse—or should I say Sadie's purse? The fabric rubbed the cement and I'm afraid it's not going to be able to be repaired.

Great. Sadie's going to kill me.

Get in line.

By the time I get home, I'm dry of emotion. I take a quick shower, washing myself clean of Dustin's scent, his love and his sex. Even when I'm clean, I remember the dirty ways he touched me and the way I always respond. Ripping that thought from my mind, I set off on foot to my mother's house, with a slight limp thanks to the bum knee.

Heading up the driveway, I squint to check if I'm seeing things correctly. This can't be! There's a note tacked onto the door. I scan the neighborhood but even the nosy neighbors are nowhere to be seen. The note is from a financial institution. This just can't be!

NOTICE OF FORECLOSURE

I call Dustin right away. "Do you think this is funny?" My voice has turned wild and hysterical, and only gets worse the more I ramble on.

"Calm down, Izzy. You're not making any sense."

"My declined cards. The stupid foreclosure notice on my mom's door. Is this supposed to be some kind of joke? Because it's not funny."

"I don't know what you're talking about. It wasn't me, Izzy. I wouldn't do that to you."

I roll my eyes. "I find that hard to believe. Even now?"

"Not ever."

My heart flutters back to life. "How is it that my money is all gone? I couldn't get my car out of the shop because the fucking mechanic is a sexist pig. I just barely scrimped by to get a bus ride home. My mom's pretty much lost her home. Has she taken all my money? What the fuck is going on, Dusty?"

My life is in shambles, and my mom—the one person that I'm used to putting all the pieces back together for me—isn't even in the country. The thought that she might be the reason for all of my issues right now hurts most.

Dustin remains very calm. "Take a picture of the notice and send it to my phone. I'll get your car out of the garage and drive it down to you. Go straight home and lock the door. I'll be there as soon as I can."

I snap a photo and text it to him, still feeling hesitant

about letting him get involved. I'm sure I'm the last person he wants to deal with at this point. "Okay, it's done, but I don't get this. Why is this happening?"

He hesitates before coming out with it. "Have you ever thought maybe Sarah married for reasons other than love? Maybe she's having money trouble."

I didn't want to believe it, but that is where all the warning signs are pointing. If I didn't know my mother better, I'd have believed it myself. But I just don't know.

"No. There's no way she's losing her house. My mother tells me everything. This isn't something she could hide from me."

"You're sure."

Even though I'd kept something from her very recently, I have to believe she wouldn't do the same. No, she couldn't have. "I know what you're thinking. She's not a gold digger, Dustin. Trust me on this one, she's not."

He sighs, hating that I catch him in his accusation. "Okay, then I'll take care of it."

"What do you mean you'll take care of it?"

"Go straight home, Izzy. I'll take care of it," he says, ending the call.

26

Mission Accomplished

I count down the minutes until my mother is due to arrive from the airport. I flash an assessing glance at the neighbor who watches me walk down the driveway and gawks the entire time I unlock the front door. That guy creeps me out, but I smile awkwardly and wave. I'm expecting my mom any minute. I assured her on the phone that I would be here when she got home, so here I am. Dustin suggested I be frank with her and that's exactly what I'm going to be.

Less than ten minutes later, my mom enters the door with a warm smile and well-loved look about her, appearing even happier than she did when she left. I hate to be the one to burst her bubble of sunshine and happiness, but I have to know the truth, and now is as good a time as ever. My mom drops her purse near the door and kicks off her shoes. She catches on instantly that something isn't right, so I get right to it.

"You're losing the house?"

She ignores my question and pulls me into a great big bear hug. "I had a wonderful, wonderful time. Thank you for asking." She rocks me side to side, still smiling.

I push her off of me. "You're avoiding the question." *Can it really be true?*

Her eyes turn hard. "You're serious?"

"Yes, mom. There was a notice on your door. Dustin took care of it, whatever that's supposed to mean. I'm sure he threw money at them and they went away. Whatever. I just can't get over that you didn't tell me."

She grips my shoulders with both her hands, her smile sliding right off her face. "Wait, Dustin did what?"

Jason walks in the room and instantly rushes to her side. "What is it?"

My mom looks to me for an answer.

"Dustin paid for the house, Mom. He settled your debt."

"Honey, just stop for a second, will you? Something's not right here." She looks directly into my eyes. "Izzabelle, what happened while we were gone?"

I look off into space, not connecting with her eyes.

"You know I don't have a mortgage on this house. It's been paid off for years. I'm afraid you've been had."

"But . . . but . . ." I can't even spit out the words. Dustin paid *someone* off, and apparently it wasn't her bank. "It looked so real. And my credit cards have been charged to the limits. I didn't want to believe it, Mom, but something is very wrong here, and if it's not you, then who?"

"Get Dustin on the phone right now," my mother tells Jason. "Where's that notice?" I cross the room, pull it out from the stack of mail and hand it to her.

"Have you had any other trouble while we've been away? Received any unusual phone calls?"

I think about it. "Nothing unusual."

"Has Dustin?" she asks Jason, but that's when it hits me.

"Janey," I whisper.

"Who?"

"Dustin's mother. She called the country club when Dustin was expecting a call, but she got me. She wasn't very pleasant and she may have threatened me a time or two." I don't want to say anymore, but I've done enough hiding from the truth. "We might have made the local news."

"Oh, Izzabelle," she groans, wondering just how bad it can be.

Jason has his hand over his eyes as Dustin fills his ear with obviously all the wrong things on the other end of the phone. "It's her, Sarah," he states, looking up at my mom.

I scrunch my nose and sneak a glance at my mom.

"There's more. Janey threatened horrible things and published them in her newspaper. Headlines, Mom. You said we could talk about this later. Maybe now's a good time. We were in the headlines for days, plastered across the front page day after day. All rumors and hearsay, of course. She put words in my mouth, made me out to be a horrible, horrible person. Then the pictures—"

Oh, the pictures are the worst of it. The one of me on my knees at the bar, Dustin crouching at my shoulder. Me exiting the pool house, in a less than dressed state, Dustin sneaking out shortly thereafter and appearing at the party with his blonde bimbo. But the worst had to be the picture taken at the clubhouse last week, unbeknownst to either of us; it's of Dustin and I sitting down to dinner, the night of the big storm. We're both gazing at each other, eyes shining. It's like his mother put that one there as a warning that there would be no more of that.

We didn't know where the photos had come from, or why someone is stalking us, but the headlines said it all. This person has set out to ruin me. Me and my mother and the Millers. I am sure the Carver Mountain Golf and Country Club will take the hit the hardest. First, they documented the fist fight, painting Rusty in a nasty light. And other, less-than-honest bystanders came forward to add their two cents about the entire ordeal. It all stemmed around me, which is still a mystery to me.

The one article was written by Dustin's mother herself. This I must tell my mother. "Janey made it sound like I'm only after Dustin for his money, because I learned that the man you married has nothing. She said that I don't think your relationship is going to last, and that's just not true."

Jason smirks at me, interrupting my emotional turmoil. "I wouldn't say I have nothing. Nothing Janey can get her filthy paws on, anyways."

"It's bad, though—so bad, Jason. Please don't believe a word of it."

"I don't believe any of the trash Janey publishes in that paper of hers. The entire thing is complete garbage. No one believes a word she says anymore."

"Just know that I never said those things about you. I know my mother married you for love, and I have the utmost respect for you and your sons."

After a long discussion that involves me telling them everything, I need air. Even with Jason's forgiveness, a little fresh air will do me a lot of good. I show myself outside and dart into the backyard, taking a seat on the huge chunk of rock I always used to sit on when I was a kid. I remember the rock holding so much warmth back then, but the cloudy day makes it so nothing feels warm.

The wind whips my hot skin, warning me to head back inside, but I need the quiet to think and so I take it. My mom peers out the window at me, but she knows when I need alone time and now is one of those times.

There's talking next door. The woman's voice is faint, but I recognize it as one of the nosy neighbors. A few words catch my ear, so I listen in for curiosity's sake. The woman doesn't realize I'm outside, or that I hear every word she says at the most critical point in her conversation.

"Yeah, they just got home this morning. I think they know something's up. They're in the house now. It's only a matter of time before they figure it out. The girl's here too."

I knew it. She's talking about me!

I slink back toward the door, careful not to attract attention to myself. I need to get closer.

"We're all loaded up. A couple more bags and we're out of here." She blows out a puff of smoke before digging her toe into the butt of the cigarette and returning inside.

I peer between the fence boards and catch the woman lifting a picnic basket off the kitchen table before disappearing farther into the house.

I sneak in my mother's back door and shut it softly. "Mom," I whisper, trying to take her attention from Jason. "Mom, I know who it was."

The pair of them stop talking on a dime and turn to me.

"It wasn't your ex-wife, Jason. It's the neighbors. They have the picnic basket."

"What are you talking about, Izzabelle? How do you know that?"

"We don't have much time. I just heard the woman on her phone. She was talking about us. They're moving out."

"It can't be."

"It can be, Mom. It is. Think about it. They moved in shortly after you started seeing Jason. They've always stalked your every move. That guy has creeped me out since the day I first saw him."

My mom's hand clasps over her open mouth, when random memories start to click into place. Jason pulls her into his arms. He presses his lips into her forehead.

"But why?" she asks, hating the feeling of being targeted.

"We'll let the authorities figure that out." Jason wastes no time calling the police with his free hand, peeking through the blinds at the neighbors, noting down their license plate number and snapping photos of their faces with his phone.

I hate to admit that I'm scared, but I am. I heard Dustin's voice on the other end of the line with Jason earlier, and it sounded like he wanted to be here to help figure out what's going on. This all happened before I took the break outside. Dustin could be here any minute and I'm not sure how I feel about that. We left things calmly, friendly even. He helped me out, just like my mom said he would. We didn't talk much about what happened between us, because all the hype kept us preoccupied and we agreed it could wait until everything died down a bit.

So much is going through my mind right now. My mom didn't lie to me, but somebody took my money. A part of me wants to be comforted, but I don't want to think about Dustin right now, or his strong arms calming me. I need to prove to him, and myself, that I can get through this alone.

"Are your boys coming over?" my mom asks.

"Dustin's on his way. So are the police."

Suddenly my fear of the neighbors and this situation disappears and I'm reminded of the unfinished conversation I had with Dustin. He must realize by now that the bullshit Janey had written about is untrue, but I'm not about to sit around to find out that I'm wrong.

"Umm, yeah, I gotta go." I rush to the door, grabbing my purse and my jacket. Despite the cold weather, I tear across the yard and jam my key in the lock.

"Izzabelle, wait!" My mother runs after me, so I quickly turn on a smile. "Is everything okay?"

"I'm fine, Mom. Let me know what happens. I'll call you when I get home."

She sighs, figuring me out all too easily. "Okay. Drive safely, honey."

"I will. Love you."

She hugs me firmly, and stares into my eyes. "Thank you for believing in me. Jason told me what Dustin said. You didn't believe it. You believed in me."

My voice is as soft as hers. "Of course I did. You're my mom."

She hugs me again. "Get out of here. We'll take care of this. Don't you worry about us. Your credit cards will be traced and our attorneys will take care of the fraudulent foreclosure notice. They're saying we're not the only case. There were others who reported finding notices on their doors in the neighborhood." She's careful to keep her back turned to the two people staring from the next door window.

But this is different, I just know it. Those other notices were just a cover. Not wanting to scare my mom, I keep my lips sealed and smile. There'll be a chance for me to tell Jason what I know in the near future.

She cups my cheek. "We'll all be okay because we have each other."

I nod and smile because I know it's true. Everything will be just fine—back to normal, if you will. The neighbors will be apprehended, Janey scorned, my mom and Jason will go back to their lovey-dovey ways and I will go back to my lonely apartment. It will all be as it was before.

I shouldn't complain. Life will be simple. I'll have my job, my friends and my books. Dustin? I'll just have to wait and see how that pans out.

27

Library Confessions

I find myself staring at my phone, longing to hear his voice just one more time. I heard Dustin in the background when I called my mom to let her know I made it home okay, but it wasn't enough. A part of me was hoping he would come groveling back to me. Wishful thinking. A man like Dustin, one of his class and charm, doesn't grovel. I don't know what I was thinking.

"Is she okay?" Dustin had asked. "Is that her? Let me talk to her." It actually sounded as if he cared. That remains to be seen.

My mom fought for the phone and didn't let him get a hold of it, and I was kind of glad then, but now I'm less than thrilled about that decision. My phone rings, sitting in the palm of my hand. My heart leaps in my chest, but it's like a gun that fired off for a false start. My face instantly falls flat. The call display doesn't lie.

I answer the phone with frustration evident in my tone. "Oh, Sadie. It's just you."

"You sound really impressed to hear from me."

I sigh, wishing my rotten attitude wasn't so obvious. "No, it's not you. It's just that I was hoping you were someone else."

"Yeah, I saw the papers. You must be talking about Dustin Miller, all hot-blooded, thick in the chest—"

My eyes widen from my equally-as-delightful memories, remembering Dustin in all his handsome glory, and then I huff when I realize that I'm the reason why we're not together right now. "—and he's gone."

It's all my fault.

"He'll be back?" she asks. "I mean, you were expecting his call, right?"

I shake my head, even though Sadie can't see me. I walk to the front window in my apartment and peer around the sheer curtain, checking the guest parking lot for the tenth time since I walked in the door.

"I don't know. I'm afraid I blew it this time, Sadie. He's not going to be calling me." My breaths come out rushed. I hope I'm not right.

Face the facts, Izzy. He's a class above you, with drive and a dream. You're just you. What do you have to offer the man who has everything? Nothing.

"Well, I'd love to say that's sad, but your loss is kind of my gain. I need you to work for me."

"I'll do it." I need an excuse to get out of this apartment and think about something other than dark eyes, a deep voice, and a bright smile.

"Thank you so much, Izzy. You start at one."

She ends the call before I can renege on my promise. I flash a glance at the time as soon as I end the call. It's already twenty after twelve.

Thanks for the notice, Sadie.

I'll have to dress quickly. It's a good thing I'm only a few minutes from my work. I throw myself together with a heavy knit sweater and black tights. It's not too cold outside that I have to wear a jacket, but it's damp enough that I had better be prepared for rain. I pull out the over-sized umbrella from the hall closet and step outside to lock up the apartment.

I round the building, trotting off as fast as I can manage, careful not to drop my purse or the umbrella in the process. I try to turn my attention onto other, less stressful things like the weather, but dark clouds roll toward me, the color of Dustin's eyes, with rain definitely on the horizon. Oh, the skies, they're so grey, much like my hope for a relationship with Dustin.

Gah! Why can't I stop thinking about him?

I look up ahead and focus on the little brick library perched on a small plot of land right in the center of town. The clouds threaten rain, but I manage to beat it by one second. For once, time is on my side. I pull on the second set of doors and slip inside, just as a crash of rain hits the ground. Sadie is at the front desk when I get there.

"Hey, lady. I thought you couldn't make it." To say I'm surprised to see her is an understatement.

"There's been a change of plans." She hesitates on what she's about to say next, not wanting to bring up the newspapers, even with a recent one glaring at me from the magazine rack. "We really need to talk. Come on. Out with it. What really happened at the country club? I can't believe you're dating that sexy beast."

I smirk, but I don't spill anything. "This is not the place for it."

"Where did you find him?"

I dare not say "in my mother's guest room", but the thought passes through my mind and I'm sure it shows on my face. But to my relief, a reader appears behind me with a book to be checked out. I shrug my shoulders and walk past the desk, but Sadie snares my gaze.

"We need to talk, just as soon as you finish up in the kids' corner. Do you mind?" Her tone is quiet and demanding. I laugh, because it looks like she's considering telling the reader to take a hike so she can ask me more about Dustin.

Smirking, I drop my purse off in the small office behind the desk. When I notice another reader lining up to check out a book, I smile at her and then head over to the kids' section to prepare for today's activities, wiggling my fingers in a teasing wave.

It's funny, we don't even open for five minutes, but these people have already managed to sneak in and find a book. Trying to beat the rain, I guess. A small group of children have already taken their seats around my favorite comfy chair, and it looks like I'm going to be the one taking care of the children's story time today.

I pick up the book that Sadie's already laid out for me and settle onto the comfy chair in the reading corner. When the clock strikes one, I waste no time making my introduction.

"Hi, kids. I'm Miss Spade, and I'll be hanging out with you for the next hour."

The kids respond with a weak, garbled attempt at, "Hi, Miss Spade," before I crack open the first book. As the hour runs on, the amount of kids dwindle, until I'm sitting there with two of them left, one lounging on either side of me.

". . . and they live happily ever after," I announce, a little relieved that the story is over.

"Will you live happily ever after?" the little girl asks me.

The mounting thunder in the distance and electricity in the air toys with my nerves. "Now, why would you ask me a thing like that?" I ask, smiling.

She shrugs her shoulders, like she's keeping a secret from me.

"Why don't you have a seat at the table and I'll get you some coloring pages?" I'm a little surprised when both the kids listen and wait eagerly for me to pick out a page for them to color.

Once I get them going, I plop down on the soft lounger again with a sigh. I pick up my own novel and find the place where I left off last week. With my finger on the spot, I take a quick glance towards the front door. The last thing I expect on this dreary excuse for a day is to catch Dustin walking through the door with the wind whipping around him, but that's exactly what I find.

Oh. My. God. He's at the library. Not just any library, but *my* library!

It's suddenly quiet—really quiet. The only sound I hear is the occasional growl of thunder and my beating heart in my ears. No one notices Dustin's approach, but my heart definitely does. It pounds passionately in my chest when I notice the bouquet of flowers in his hand. Am I imagining this?

I glance up at him from my book and the two kids who

were coloring are now looking at Sadie. She signals for them to scoot. They both get up from the table and run off, leaving me trembling in my seat.

Dustin pulls off his hat as a sign of respect. Inwardly, I swoon, before he's even noticed me sitting there. He glances around at the tall rows of book shelves and at the poster on the wall, as he makes a hesitant approach toward the front desk. I know the minute Sadie notices she has company. Her eyes flash up to greet him, expressing just how often we get the big, buff model-type walking in the front door.

After waiting his turn, behind a boy half his size, he smiles at Sadie. "Hi. I'm looking for Izzabelle Spade," he tells her.

I can barely hear him, but his deep voice resonates in the room and sends a shiver through my body, pulse racing. My eyes fall closed as I try to fend off my nerves and attraction. When my eyes flutter open, he's staring at me from across the room, standing there very still and very quiet. I feel like the hunted, frozen in place, praying that I've not been had.

After a couple of blinks, he follows the direction of Sadie's pointed finger and that brings him in my direction. He doesn't take his eyes off me as he slowly stalks closer. My book remains open on my lap, my ankles crossed and leaned to one side. I think I might pee my pants.

He stops next to me and presents me with flowers. I do my best to restrain my elation as I breathe in their fresh scent and then rest them next to my feet. I consider jumping up and diving into those strong arms, hanging on for dear life this time, but I do my best cool expression and wait for him to say something.

"Do you have a minute?"

My heart soars. I gesture for him to take a seat, even though he's much too large to feel comfortable in any of the small chairs I've pointed to. Still, he pulls out the small orange one and sits his perfect little ass on it. I can't help but smirk when he raises his eyebrows in disbelief.

I can't believe he fits, either!

Smirking, I ask him, "What are you doing here?" My voice

comes out so softly that no one else can hear me. Years in the library system has rendered me expert at private conversations in public.

"You tell me," he insists, like he's just as mystified by his visit.

I shrug a coy shoulder, loving the way his smile plays on his lips.

"I want to be with you." Dustin's voice is firm and slices the air like a hot knife through butter. He knows exactly what he's doing here, and so do I.

I lose all sense of time and place. It's just him—all brooding and sexy—and me, completely mute. The urgency in his voice kicks at my heart. He watches the emotions play across my face.

"I've treated you badly. I know I apologized and figured you could use some time to find forgiveness—" His eyes hone in on mine, his voice no less potent. "That was a mistake. Time isn't what you need, and I'm done waiting."

I'm smiling up at him now, but I'm speechless. What is he saying?

"I want to be with you, Izzy."

I snap my book shut and scramble to my feet, pressing a finger against his lips. "Shh." I take him by the elbow and help him to his feet. He struggles for a second, knocking aside the small chair, as rain begins to crash off the nearby window. He reaches for my hand and pulls me into the maze of shelves, leaving me breathless and backed into a wall of books. I rest a hand on one of the upper shelves behind me for support and tilt my head upwards. He slowly leans forward until our foreheads are touching, and he too closes his eyes.

"I never said those things about your dad," I say.

"I know you didn't." Dustin takes my chin between his fingers, and gently lifts it, his warm breath washing over my lips. I think he's going to kiss me, but he doesn't. He's waiting for my eyes to meet his before he admits something. But what?

"I have something for you. But you have to say yes." He

cracks open a little box, before I even realize he's holding one.

I gasp. "What is this?"

He holds it up to me. "This is a promise ring. I miss you, Izzabelle. I'm done missing you. This ring will ensure that I always listen to you and that you will always smack me up when I'm wrong. Your mom was pretty happy with my idea. I even have my father's blessing. There's only one person I'm waiting to hear from." He pauses, like this person will be the determining force.

"Who?" I wonder.

He smiles back at me. "It's you, Izzabelle. I want you to wear my ring. I promise to believe in you in all things. That is, if you still want me."

My eyelashes flutter frantically when he slides the ring onto my finger. "I love it. Yes! Of course I want you."

He reaches into his back pocket and I see that today he's come bearing another gift. First, he hands me a pencil. I stare at it, wondering about its significance. It looks like an ordinary yellow pencil, sharpened at one end, flat on the other. . . I soon figure it out.

Tears well in my eyes as he loops his arms around mine and pulls me flush to his body.

"Most pencils have erasers," he starts. "But not this one. I don't want to forget what we've shared. You shouldn't forget, either."

"I'll never forget," I say wistfully, smiling into his eyes and clutching my new pencil.

The way he stares at my lips, I know he wants to kiss me, but he abstains. "You really have no idea how beautiful you are—smart, kind, funny.

Dustin makes me blush and smirk at once, but there remains one very large elephant in the room. "Your dad married my mom. You sure you're okay with that?"

He becomes defensive, but mostly just passionate—about me. "I don't care if our parents live together. Who really fucking cares?"

I slap my hand over his mouth, dropping my jaw in

surprise. "Watch your mouth," I warn, like a naughty librarian who will punish him if he doesn't listen.

He smirks and kisses my hand, pulling it away to finish his sentence. "Our parents are married. Good for them. They've given me their approval. Do I care what others think? No. That means nothing to me, Izzabelle. You—you mean something to me."

A tear trickles down my smiling cheek. "You make me feel so special. I'm actually pretty ordinary. I don't go out much—not to the movies, not to the gym."

"I want you," he states, without question in his voice. "And I'm not going to stop wanting you, even if you wipe your teary eyes all over my shirt and hang your smelly socks in my bathroom."

"I don't have smelly socks," I squawk, making the kids around the corner snicker.

Dustin continues to profess his devotion to me. "All I'm saying is, I love you. I'll do my part if you'll do yours. But I need you to say yes—yes, you'll be mine, yes, we can be together." His eyes burn into mine with an electric force.

"Yes."

Dustin smiles wider than I've ever seen before, and tilts his head, inching slowly toward me, not caring who's watching. He takes my mouth against his, tasting me, burying his hands in my hair, ignoring the giggling children around the corner of the bookshelf. His public affection exposes his feelings more than anything else could, his fervent kiss turning slow and meaningful. This all feels too good to be true. Dustin is everything I ever wanted in a man and more.

"I love you."

He kisses me again and smiles. "I knew it."

Surrounded by my two favorite things in this world, my books and my man, I whisper to him. "I can't believe this is really happening."

He glances down at me through half-lidded eyes, regarding me in his arms like a cherished angel, pausing only to say, "Tough cookies." He collects me closer, smiling radiantly into my soul. The stormy swirl in his eyes softens, as he drops down for another kiss—one of many more to come.

The End

Support This Author

LEAVE A REVIEW!

GOODREADS
www.goodreads.com/christasimpson

OTHER CHANNELS
www.christasimpson.com/tough-luck

Please sign up for Christa's readers' list to receive special news, sneak previews and exclusive offers from Author Christa Simpson!

http://eepurl.com/brKtgL

About the Author

Christa Simpson is a Bestselling Romance Author who entertains her readers with protective alpha males and sassy heroines. She writes sexy new adult romances loaded with passion, suspense and sarcasm. In her free time, she loves reading, writing, music, movies and dancing.

Christa is a small town girl living in Chatham-Kent, Ontario, with her husband and two beautiful daughters. She's a dreamer and has always believed you can do anything you set your mind to.

Please visit her website:
WWW.CHRISTASIMPSON.COM

Author of . . .

THE TWISTED SERIES
Book 1: Twisted
Book 2: Twist & Turn
Book 3: A Twist of Fate
Book 4: Twisted Desire

THE DESTINY SERIES
Book 1: Finding Destiny
Book 2: Beautifully Broken
Book 3: Perfectly Ruined

TOUGH LUCK (A Stepbrother Romance)

A Note from the Author

Hey, you. Thanks for reading my book. I hope you liked it, because I had a hell of a lot of fun writing it. Can you believe this book started out as a short story that wasn't supposed to exceed 6,000 words? Oopsy! Lol.

Needless to say, I wasn't ready to leave these characters alone and so I wrote up a plan to turn Tough Luck into a full blown story. I'm still feeling a little sad to let these two go so soon. I'll admit it stings a little. This is my first single title romance after all. It's true! Twisted Desire does stand alone, but if you've read the Twisted Trilogy then you know Aliah was a secondary character from Twisted. The books in the Destiny series standalone too, but I get to drag all those characters' butts back into the next story in the series. I can't wait to show you how I've pulled them all together in Perfectly Ruined, which is coming soon. If you like your firemen smoking hot—like I do—then you won't want to miss it.

On a separate note, I would love to hear how you like it. Yeah, keep your mind in the gutter. I've been flip-flopping back and forth between less steamy versions of the stories I'm telling and flat out erotica. Tell me, what heat level are you looking for in your next book? Did you find this story mild or was it pushing your boundaries?

Thanks again for reading and I look forward to seeing you at the end of my next book!

Did you know I'm always looking for people just like you to join my team of readers? If you'd like to know about my upcoming books and promotions, please subscribe to my newsletter at http://eepurl.com/brKtgL.

Never miss out on any updates by following my blog at www.christasimpson.com/blog, or by visiting me on Facebook at www.facebook.com/authorchristasimpson.

I also have a very cool Facebook group called Christa Simpson's Twisted Sisters where I hang out on occasion and talk books with some crazy fun ladies. If you visit Facebook, request to join and we'll add you!

If you enjoyed this book, please consider leaving a review. Even if you hate writing reviews, know that nothing elaborate is required. Reviews are incredibly important to indie authors like me and I'd appreciate it so much if you took a moment to leave one.

Acknowledgements

Okay, I'd like to drop a quick thanks or three before I go.

To my right-hand woman, my bestie, my beta, my everything. How many times can I thank a single person, but you really are my SFAM. I always trust your opinion, rely on you to give it to me real, and love that I have a virtual shoulder to lean on whenever I need one. We will meet in person someday soon. I promise!

To Jaz, my editor. What a relief to know you have my back. I'm confident you will catch all those pesky words that I fly right over, time and time again. I'm sorry for being so comma happy this time around, but I'm glad you were able to fix this baby right up. Just know that I appreciate your expertise and look forward to working with you again in the future.

I'm happy to announce that my pimping queen has been promoted to the book pimping momma! Congrats Melissa Crump on the new addition to your family. The fact that you still find time to show your support so regularly truly does not go unnoticed. Thank you!

To you . . . yeah, you! Thank you so much for taking the time to read my story. You might have noticed that I sprinkle myself all over social media, so don't be a stranger. I'm always happy to interact with my readers. Hope to see you over there!

Christa Simpson

OTHER TITLES BY THIS AUTHOR
The Twisted Series

The Destiny Series

BWPbooks.com

BWP

HTTP://CHRISTASIMPSON.COM

TWISTED

Can a man and woman be just friends?

Have a look at Christa Simpson's debut release!

After graduating from law school with honours, Edwin Santora, Abigail's occasional ex and handsome housemate, could get a job anywhere he wants. Of all the places to land, why does he take a position with her small firm? As if sharing a house with her irresistible ex isn't bad enough, it quickly becomes the least of her concerns. When Edwin's macho arrogance begins to seriously affect her dating life, Abigail starts to reconsider their friendship; not that Edwin believes a man and woman can be "just friends" anyway.

With Edwin's swoon-worthy stunts and fierce persistence, Abigail finds herself catching feelings. When Edwin makes a friendly proposal, no-strings-attached, Abigail can't resist.

After some sexy role playing, she finds herself dangerously in love and wrapped back up in Edwin's powerful grip. When Abigail risks everything, revealing a treacherous little secret, will their friendship pass the test? Or will they give in to the mysterious forces trying to drive them apart?

www.christasimpson.com/twisted

THE DESTINY SERIES: BOOK 1

FINDING DESTINY

Skylar has rules. Destiny has him breaking every last one of them.

Destiny is looking forward to a bit of solitude in the north to beat away the winter blues. That's the plan. Destiny likes plans. But plans don't always work out the way you want them to.

Skylar never expects to find three ladies trudging through the snow, stranded, in the middle of nowhere, during the biggest snow storm of the year. He's forced to invite Destiny and her friends back to his cabin. Though he tries to ignore what is subtly unravelling between them, he can't discount their attraction. The way Destiny reads into his thoughts and the way his jealousy rages at the thought of his brother taking her to his bed, he knows he had better stake his claim.

But when tragedy strikes, torn from her arms at lightning speed, Skylar's left to wonder whether he will ever find his destiny.

www.christasimpson.com/finding-destiny

The Destiny cast returns in . . .

PERFECTLY RUINED

www.christasimpson.com/perfectly-ruined

Black Widow
Publishing

www.pinterest.com/BWPbooks
www.twitter.com/blackwidowpub
www.facebook.com/blackwidowpublishing

Kill your competition with Black Widow Publishing!

www.ingramcontent.com/pod-product-compliance
Lightning Source LLC
Chambersburg PA
CBHW020951180626
46814CB00003B/1044